MYSTERY OF THE TEA CUP QUILT

HARLAND CREEK MYSTERY QUILTERS (A COZY MYSTERY)

JODI ALLEN BRICE

Copyright © 2022 by Jodi Allen Brice

All rights reserved.

No part of this book may be reproduced in any form or by any electronic or mechanical means, including information storage and retrieval systems, without written permission from the author, except for the use of brief quotations in a book review.

❦ Created with Vellum

This book is dedicated to Jana from Jana's Quilting in Jonesboro Arkansas. When I saw her spectacular tea cup quilt, I knew I had a mystery brewing in my head. Please check out her facebook page Jana's Quilting and tell her Jodi sent you!

CHAPTER 1

I pulled into the parking spot in front of Mildred's Quilt Shop and killed the engine of my car. The Ford Taurus sputtered twice, blew out a plume of smoke, and finally gave up the ghost and died.

My shoulders slumped forward as the weight of the world came crashing down on me.

How had I ended up back here?

I had once been on top of the world, living a life most dreamed of.

Instead of heading off to college, I'd moved to New York right after high school and built my business from the ground up. It took only a few short years to become a success of designing and selling children's clothes. I was the brains behind the brand, Catherine Lecroix. I had a luxurious apartment near Central Park, friends who adored me, and was dating Jacques Bellin, the French heir to a prestigious vineyard in France.

I had done the impossible. I had made it all happen. Until it was all ripped away.

One mistake of bringing in a business partner, Cal Rapport, resulted in me losing everything. My business, my reputation, my dream. Cal had talked me into changing manufacturer and distributor when business was booming. He said they could handle all the bulk orders I had coming in. I was skeptical at first, because I didn't want to scrimp on quality. He assured me that the manufacturer would adhere to my standards. So I relented. Within months we were making money, hand over fist, and I was thrilled.

Until the DEA came knocking on my door. I quickly found out that Cal had been smuggling drugs in my children's clothes. He was tipped off about the bust and had taken all the money and left the United States.

I was left holding the bag. While the DEA realized I had nothing to do with the criminal activity, they said they were going to keep a close eye on me. Which meant I had to keep my nose clean, pun intended.

I had hit rock bottom and was back in Harland Creek. I was living with my mom, Mildred Agnew, and owner of Mildred's Quilt shop, my New York friends had ghosted me, and Louie had ended our relationship.

The only saving grace from my humiliation was that no one knew how far I had fallen because I had built my success under a brand name. I had planned on telling my mom all I had accomplished once I sold the business to an interested party. I wanted to have enough funds so she would never have to worry about money again. She could retire from working and finally enjoy life.

I thought no one knew my secret. But I was wrong.

Yesterday, Gertrude Brown had come into the quilt shop demanding that I finish her quilt in one day. I'd never liked that old lady. She was as mean as a snake and cruel just for sport. I had let my anger get the best of me and let Gertrude have a piece of my mind. My mom had been horrified and the two customers in the store had gaped.

I immediately regretted my action and tried to apologize, but Gertrude stormed out of the store. My guilt had me staying late after the quilt shop closed to try to finish her quilt as a peace offering. I should have known better. There would never be any peace between Gertrude Brown and me.

Things went from bad to worse when Gertrude burst into the quilt shop after Mom had left. Gertrude told me she knew about my secret in New York. She said she would not hesitate to tell the whole town I was a criminal if I didn't finish quilting her Tea Cup quilt that night. Gertrude was the cruelest woman in Harland Creek, bent on making everyone miserable if she didn't get her way.

I laid my head on the steering wheel and groaned. "Why didn't I just keep my big mouth shut?"

A knock on my car window jolted me back to the cruel reality of where I was.

I frowned at the plump older woman with mousy

brown hair styled in a bowl cut. She shoved her vintage silver glitter cat eye glasses up on the bridge of her nose and squinted at me. She was wearing a tight purple tracksuit in the middle of summer. The stress lines around her mouth and forehead made me think she was in her late fifties.

I went to press the button to roll down the window, then remembered I was no longer in my Lexus convertible.

Grimacing, I remembered the Ford's windows couldn't be rolled down without turning the engine back on. I didn't want to deal with another fart of smoke so I opened the door.

"Yes?" I asked.

"You must be Dove Agnew. You're Mildred's daughter, aren't you?" The woman's mouth shot up in a wide grin, making her cheeks look big and rosy. "I could tell by the eyes. No one has eyes like Mildred."

I cringed at the sound of my birth name but then forced a smile. It had been a while since anyone called me Dove.

"I am."

"I'm Patricia Earle. I work with your mom. She hired me a few months ago to help in the quilt shop. I was off these last few days to take care of Mother. She schedules all her doctor's appointments the same week and I have to drive her." Her smile faltered. "Mildred said you'd be working here, too."

I sighed and nodded slowly. "Yes. Mom asked me to

help with the quilting orders. Seems like summer is a busy few months for her."

Patricia looked a little pale around the lips. "So, you will not be running the register? I was afraid you were going to replace me." She extracted an inhaler from the pocket of her tracksuit, put it to her mouth and took a deep pull.

I frowned. "Are you okay?" The last thing I needed was to be giving a strange woman CPR.

She nodded and then let out the breath. "Yes. I have asthma. My mom told me I don't need to get all worked up and upset over nothing."

"Your mom is right."

"She's always telling me what to do. I live with her." She gave me a slight smile. "Like you and Mildred."

My smile slid off my face. "It's only temporary." Like me, staying in Harland Creek was temporary.

She smiled. "That's what I said. But it's been ten years since I moved back home, and I'm still living with my mom. I'll see you inside." She gave a little finger wave and walked into the quilt shop.

It was my first week back at Mom's quilt shop, and I already felt like I was suffocating.

I glanced at my reflection in the rearview mirror. The double braid I had fashioned my blonde hair into was starting to frizz in the Mississippi heat. I blinked. Patricia had been right.

No one had ice blue eyes like my Mom, except me.

Instead of wallowing in my self-pity, I climbed out of my car and grabbed my Christian Louboutin bag, the only expensive thing I still owned, and made my way to the shop.

The honeysuckle that wrapped around the side of the building hung heavy in the air. A smile escaped my lips, reminding me of sweet memories of how as a child, I'd pluck the blossoms and suck on the nectar.

A bead of sweat trickled from my neck down my back. I had sold a lot of my expensive clothes back in New York and my wardrobe was severely limited. Thankfully I'd borrowed a T-shirt of Mom's and my denim shorts to help stay cool while I quilted. While the shop had air conditioning, the room where I worked was the hottest in the building.

I swiped my brow with the back of my hand and opened the door to the quilt shop.

Patricia had already switched the window sign to Open and had turned on all the lights. The scent of fabric welcomed me inside the shop as I made my way toward the back room where the long arm machine was.

The phone rang, and Patricia immediately answered. "Mildred's Quilt Shop, where the sewing magic happens. How may I help you?"

I headed to the back room and put my purse under the counter where my mom kept the coffee maker beside the usual tray of pastries that her quilting buddies would bring by.

My mom poked her head out of the office. "Good morning, Dove. I was hoping you'd get here earlier so you can work on Gertrude Brown's quilt. She left two messages on the answering machine after we closed. After that terrible row between you two, I think it best if we go ahead and finish her quilt." Mom let out a heavy sigh.

"I'm sorry about what I said to her yesterday. I know it's not good for business to be yelling at customers. No matter how demanding they are." I gave her a pained smile.

"Well, she had it coming. No one has ever stood up to her in this town." Mom shook her head. "I swear this is the last time I'm ever quilting for her."

I poured myself a cup of black coffee and walked over to her. "I finished her quilt last night."

My mom's eyebrows shot up in surprise. "You what?"

"I stayed up half the night so I could finish it. I even completed the binding."

Mom gaped. "That's the quickest quilting job I've ever seen."

"I wasn't going to stay late, but after what happened yesterday, I felt it best to get it done." I left out the part about Gertrude trying to blackmail me.

Mom stood up and her eyebrows knit together in a frown. "That woman is so demanding. And mean as a snake to boot." She lifted her chin. "You should have just made her wait. I would have if she had talked to me that way."

I took a sip of my coffee and averted my eyes. "I didn't mind," I lied. I minded a lot.

Mom pressed her lips together in a thin line. "That

woman thinks she runs Harland Creek. I don't like people like that."

"Neither do I. Want me to call to tell her to come get her quilt?" I looked at her.

"Let me see it first. I don't want to give that old bat something to criticize." Mom set her mug of coffee down on the counter and followed me out of the office.

"Knock, knock!" The woman I recognized as Elizabeth Harland, walked into the back of the shop. Gray, short hair curtaining a face with kind, yet strong features, Elizabeth Harland was a steel magnolia. She sought comfort over fashion and worked hard for a living. She wore blue jeans and a floral blouse with black orthopedic shoes with white socks. "I brought goodies. Homemade lemon bars. My grandmother's recipe." She held up the decorative platter covered in cellophane.

Elizabeth Harland was one of Mom's quilting group. She was widowed, ran her own flower farm with a young woman named Heather, and the town was named after her ancestors. She preferred muumuus when she worked her farm and was a wonderful cook.

Mom walked over to give her friend and fellow quilting buddy a hug. "Elizabeth, you shouldn't have. But I'm glad you did." She turned to me. "You remember my daughter, Dove?"

Elizabeth gave me a bright smile. "Of course, I do. Hello, Dove. So nice to have you back in Harland Creek."

I smiled in spite of myself. "Thank you, Mrs. Harland. I'm here to help Mom get caught up on her long arm quilting."

"That's right. You're quite the seamstress." She walked over and placed the platter of sweets next to the coffee. "And please call me, Elizabeth. I hope you'll join us for our quilting bee. We'd love to have the help. We have to finish hand quilting a quilt of valor for one of the residents at the nursing home."

"How kind of you. But I don't know if you'll want me quilting with you ladies. I'm better at long arm quilting than hand quilting."

"I doubt that." Elizabeth gave me a wink. "Have you had time to finish a quilt yet? I'd love to see it."

"Then you got here in time. She finished Gertrude's last night. Fastest quilting job I've ever seen." Mom shook her head.

"I heard she made some kind of coffee pot quilt." Elizabeth wrinkled her nose.

I let out a laugh. "Actually, it's a tea cup quilt. She appliqued fabrics in the shape of tea cups and tea pots onto her blocks."

"Sounds pretty. Which is unlike Gertrude." Elizabeth groused.

"Oh, it is pretty. She even added folded vintage women's handkerchiefs under each tea cup. She sewed a seam around the whole handkerchief so it wouldn't open. The effect was pretty, but it made it difficult to quilt through the extra layers."

"If she were going to do that, she should have just cut the handkerchief in half." Elizabeth quipped.

"I totally agree, and I told her that. Her response was to shut up and sew it the way she wanted."

Mom gasped. "Dove, you should have called me. I don't let anyone talk to my employees, let alone, my daughter like that."

"I heard you gave Gertrude quite an earful yesterday." Elizabeth grinned.

"Ugh. I guess it's all over town. I was hoping to avoid that." I buried my face in my hands.

"Ha! That old bird had it coming." Elizabeth lifted her chin. "Hopefully you won't have to deal with her again."

I took another sip of my coffee. "I hope not. Come on, I'll show you the finished product."

Mom and Elizabeth followed me into the next room, where we kept the quilt orders written on a whiteboard. There was a wall of built-in shelves where we kept the pieced quilts to be quilted, as well as the finished quilts waiting to be picked up.

I flicked on the switch and immediately screamed.

A body, with lifeless eyes stared up at me.

Lying in the middle of the white linoleum floor was Gertrude Brown.

Dead.

CHAPTER 2

I rested my head on the cool surface of Mom's desk and squeezed my eyes shut. It felt like an eternity since the police arrived to examine the scene.

"You poor thing. How's your head? You were out a good five minutes when you fainted." Patricia pressed a mug of hot coffee into my hands as I sat in the chair at Mom's desk.

"Your mom said it must have been the blood that caused you to faint."

I grimaced at the memory and looked up at Patricia. "Have the police questioned you yet?" I took a sip and grimaced at the bitter coffee.

Patricia took a pull on her inhaler. "Yes, but they didn't seem so interested in what I had to say, since I didn't find the body."

My heartbeat thumped loudly in my chest. I had

found the body. And I was the one who'd yelled at Gertrude in front of witnesses.

This wasn't looking good for me.

"Dove, I think Sloan is ready to question you." Mom stepped into the office with Elizabeth and Agnes Jackson behind her wearing overalls and a large brim hat. I could almost swear a honey bee was sitting on the top. Agnes owned a ton of bee hives and was doing well selling her honey along with other items made with it.

As soon as the police were called, Elizabeth called Agnes. She and half the quilting ladies showed up before the police arrived.

I set my coffee down on the desk and tried to still my trembling hands. "Where is he?"

"Out front, by the register. Oh, and stay away from the window. Albert Jones, the photographer from the newspaper, is out there trying to get pictures." Agnes patted my arm. "And don't say something that will incriminate you or your mother."

"Incriminate? We are both innocent." I gave the woman wearing a wide brim hat an incredulous look.

"And that's exactly what you keep saying. And I wouldn't bring up the argument you had with Gertrude before she died." Sylvia Jenkins, part-owner of the S&M beauty shop, which was short for Sylvia and Maggie, spoke up. Sylvia was stylishly dressed in black slacks, white blouse and her short blonde hair was perfectly coiffed. She usually wore ballet flats since she was on her feet all the time. Sylvia had arrived with

Lorraine Chisolm. Sylvia had just put Lorraine's hair in rollers when she'd gotten the news from Agnes. They wasted no time, but jumped in the car and drove straight over.

Lorraine patted her forehead with the towel still draped around her shoulders. Despite being retired from nursing, she wore green scrubs over her thin frame with crocs. She said she'd spent half her life in scrubs and didn't intend on stopping now since they were so comfortable. "I know an excellent lawyer, just in case." Lorraine nodded.

"Thanks, but I'm innocent, Lorraine. I had no reason to kill that woman." I shook my head.

"She's right. The problem is half the town has already heard about the argument you had with her in the shop yesterday." Bertha Mills appeared at Sylvia's elbow with a lemon bar. "Gertrude Brown was mean as a snake. Half the town couldn't stand her." She shoved half the bar in her mouth and chewed. Bertha wore a puke green muumuu and some ugly black shoes. Her salt and pepper hair was sticking up all over the place due to the humidity. Bertha was not known for her pleasant disposition, and I had often wondered why the other quilting ladies tolerated her.

"Bertha's right, which is rare." Agnes nodded. Bertha gave her a scowl and tried to talk but ended up choking on the lemon bar. Agnes hit her hard on the back, making half the lemon bar go skidding across the floor.

My stomach dropped. "I didn't do anything to that woman."

"Of course you didn't, honey." Agnes patted her arm. "That's exactly what you're going to tell the police."

I flinched and tried to focus on something else. Anything else. "I hope this doesn't take long. I need to get started on the next quilt."

"Dove? I need to ask you some questions." Sloan Jackson poked his head in the office's door.

"Hi Sloan." Sylvia and Lorraine gave the officer a smile and a delicate finger wave.

"Hello, ladies. I need to speak with Dove." He zeroed his gaze on me.

"I'm coming." I got to my feet and followed Sloan into the front of the store.

Instead of pulling out a pen and notepad, he propped his hands on his hips and studied me. "How are you doing, Dove? I didn't know you were back in town." Sloan was a few years younger than me so we didn't exactly grow up together.

"Yeah. I'm here to help Mom catch up on her quilting." It wasn't a total lie.

"You found the body, correct?" Sloan cocked his head.

"Yes. Mom and I. And Elizabeth was in the shop, too." I swallowed hard. "It was quite shocking." I admitted.

Another officer walked up. "Sloan, the police chief

is here. He said he wanted to question the suspect himself."

I held my hands up in a defensive gesture. "Wait, am I a suspect?"

Sloan shrugged. "Everyone is a suspect until cleared. It's just a formality."

He drew his attention away from me to the front door. "Hey Chief. I was just about to question, Dove…"

"Dove Agnew."

I almost gasped at the familiar male voice. In that moment, I glanced down at my faded jeans shorts and old pink T-shirt with the words "Women are like Bacon. We look good, taste good, but will slowly kill you."

I closed my eyes in dread. Why had I worn this T-shirt of all mornings?

Of all the times to run into my high school sweetheart, a murder scene was the worst.

I forced a smile and slowly turned around. His dark black hair and turquoise blue eyes were just as stunning and dreamy as I remembered in high school. The only thing that had changed were the tiny lines around his eyes, which had probably come with the stress of the job. "Dean Gray. I didn't know you were the chief of police at Harland Creek." My eyes scanned his uniform and my heart skipped a beat at the sight of him.

A slight grin played at the corner of his mouth. "Only been Chief for a year now. Doing my part to keep the peace in Harland Creek." He cocked his head.

"We haven't had a murder in a while. You seem to be livening things up around the small town."

My eyes grew wide as I pressed my lips into a thin line. I felt my anger flooding my cheeks. "Dean, I had nothing to do with this. I hardly knew that woman."

"So I hear." He nodded toward a small corner of the store, away from the window. "Let's talk over there." He looked back at Sloan. "Tell the coroner to let me know the cause of death ASAP and get Albert away from the window. He's not allowed to take photos of an active crime scene."

Sloan laughed. "I'll try, but Albert is trying to impress you with his photography skills. Says he's getting bored working at the newspaper. He thinks working for the police is more his speed."

Dean shook his head. "Albert has one speed. Turtle." He looked back at me. "Let's talk."

I followed him to the corner where the wall of colorful spools of thread was on display on the wall.

When he turned around, his expression was stern as he withdrew a pen and pad out of his uniform pocket. "When did you arrive in Harland Creek?"

"A couple of weeks ago."

"Have you been working for your mom the entire time?" He narrowed his eyes.

"No. I took some time off to get settled in. I just started working this week." I lifted my chin. "You don't seriously think I had anything to do with that old woman's death."

He lifted his shoulders in a slow shrug. "You'll be surprised at what people are capable of."

Anger flooded my veins. "Now, you look here. I didn't do anything to Gertrude."

"Is it true she came by the shop yesterday and you two got into an argument?"

"Yes." I crossed my arms over my chest. "She was very rude and demeaning... and well my mouth got the better of me."

He narrowed his eyes. "What did you two argue about?"

"She wanted me to finish the quilt she brought in. She just brought it in yesterday. I told her it would take a couple of days. But she insisted I finish it last night."

Dean ran his fingers through his hair. "Gertrude was always stubborn."

"She even came into the quilt shop after it was closed. I know I locked the door but somehow she got in."

He frowned. "You were here last night?"

"Yes." I sighed heavily. "After the row we got into, I decided to stay late to finish the quilt. I hoped it would make up for the argument."

"Gertrude wouldn't have forgiven you. She was a stubborn woman." Dean shook his head.

"Dean, stop being nice. Gertrude had enemies all over town." Agnes had eased up behind me and narrowed her eyes at him.

Elizabeth walked up right beside her friend.

Agnes pointed her finger at Dean. "Gertrude was a

snake and a thief. Why she stole my bees last spring, and no one on the police force did a dang thing about it. I'm surprised someone didn't knock her in the head before now."

"I'm not sure how someone can steal bees." Dean narrowed his eyes at Agnes and Elizabeth. "I'm trying to interrogate the witness, Mrs. Jackson. Do you mind?"

"Go right ahead, dear." Elizabeth smiled. "I just need to pick out some thread for my quilt." She turned her attention to the wall and slowly perused the spools.

Dean gritted his teeth and grabbed my elbow, urging me a few steps away from the nosy quilters.

I gave him my full attention. "I didn't do anything."

"Dove, you are the last person to see her alive."

"That's not true. The last person to see her alive was the murderer." I crossed my arms over my chest and smirked.

"Exactly." His eyes hardened. "Until I solve this case, don't leave town."

My smirk slid off my face. My heart squeezed in pain.

Dean actually thought I was a suspect.

"I don't have any other place to go," I muttered.

His gaze drifted down to my shirt, read the words, and rolled his eyes before walking away.

"Don't worry, honey. We believe you." Elizabeth walked up beside me and squeezed my arm.

At least someone thought I was innocent.

CHAPTER 3

"So the police say no one is allowed back in until after they finish gathering evidence." I swiped a bead of sweat off the back of my neck with my hand and looked at the yellow tape around the quilt shop.

"Go home, Patricia. I'm sure we'll be closed at least through the weekend." Mom looked at Patricia.

Patricia's eyes went wide and her lip trembled. "I have to work, Mildred. I have to help pay for Mother's medical bills." Her breathing grew faster. Grabbing her inhaler out of her pocket, she took a deep pull.

"Relax, Patricia. This won't be forever. We'll be back open really soon. Now go home and I'll call you when I know something." Mom patted her arm reassuringly.

Patricia calmed down and headed toward her older model minivan.

"I'll leave my car and ride with you." I looked at Mom

Once we arrived home, we assembled in the kitchen. I started a pot of coffee while Mom sat at the oak kitchen table staring straight ahead.

"This is just so surreal." Mom shook her head. "I've never had anyone die in my quilt shop before."

I pulled down two mugs from the cabinet and set them beside the coffee pot. Before I could finish grabbing the cream out of the refrigerator, there was a knock at the door.

"I'll get it." Before I made it out of the kitchen, Agnes was leading the quilting ladies and a small goat into the house.

"Don't bother getting the door, Dove. We always let ourselves in." Agnes patted my arm before passing me on her way into the kitchen.

"Hello, Dove." Maggie Rowe, the other part-owner of the S&M beauty salon, gave me a smile and hurried into the kitchen with a plastic container of what I assumed was something sweet and homemade. Maggie had her dark brown hair cut in a stylish bob. She was wearing a long summer dress with beaded sandals.

"Hello, again, Dove," Elizabeth smiled and filed into the kitchen along with the small goat wearing a pink collar. The animal was desperately trying to chew through the rope attached to her collar as she followed behind Elizabeth.

Weenie Dunst must have seen my expression because she leaned closer and said in a whispered voice, "It's okay. Elizabeth is babysitting Petunia. She's house trained so she won't go potty inside."

"Oh. Good." I frowned.

Weenie was a thin slip of a woman who was a retired librarian who sometimes worked part-time at the English Rose Bookstore. She always wore clothes two sizes too large. At the moment she wore baggy jeans and an oversize T-shirt with sneakers. Her curly white hair went wild in the humidity.

"Hello, Dove." Donna Williams, my retired high school computer teacher, stood in front of me with a sad smile. "How are you holding up, honey?"

I swallowed the painful lump that appeared in the back of my throat. "I'm not sure."

I didn't know what to say. Mrs. Donna had always been my favorite teacher and had listened to all my hopes and dreams when I had been a student. She always encouraged all her students to strive to achieve their dream. I hadn't seen her in years. Suddenly, she was in front of me and all I felt was shame on top of the rest of the day's events.

"Why don't we go outside to get some fresh air?" She gently took my elbow and walked me to the front porch while pulling a small cooler bag on wheels.

The summer heat smacked me in the face like a wet rag, and I sucked in a deep breath.

"Let's sit on the swing." Donna led me to the swing at the end of the front porch and we both sat. "I think we could use some of this." She bent to unzip the cooler and pulled a large mason jar of what looked like lemonade and two plastic cups.

She unscrewed the top and began filling the two cups. "You're not watching your sugar intake, are you?"

"Nope. Is that your homemade lemonade that you used to bring to class?" The memories of Mrs. Donna passing out cups of lemonade at the end of May, before school was out for the summer, were some of my most vivid. She was the only teacher who did that.

"Absolutely." She handed me a cup, then screwed the lid back on the jar and put it in the cooler. Sitting back with her own cup, we both sipped quietly.

"I guess you know what happened?" I cut my eyes at her.

"I heard the rumors, but I'd like to hear from you." Mrs. Donna looked straight ahead.

"I went to show Mom and Elizabeth the quilt I finished for Gertrude. That's when we found her in the room with the quilts."

"I don't like to speak ill of the dead, but that Gertrude was one of the meanest women I'd ever known. There's not many people that are sad she's gone. It's kind of like a weight has been lifted off the town."

"I remember as a child, she caught me taking a shortcut on her land to the creek. She started shooting at me with a shotgun." The words fell out of my mouth. I'd never told anyone that story.

Donna's eyes bulged as she stared at me. "She tried to shoot you? Didn't the police do anything about it?"

"I didn't tell anyone. I was the one trespassing." I

shrugged. "Since I'm the one that found her, the police think I'm a suspect."

"Gertrude had enemies. The police will check out all potential suspects." Donna set the swing in motion with her foot. "Elizabeth said you got into an argument with her at the shop."

"Yes. And I'm sure half the town knows about it."

Donna smiled. "Well, it is a small town." She looked out over the tree lined street. "Was that the last time you saw her? When you had the argument?"

"She came by after we were closed. I forgot to lock the door after we closed and she let herself in. She told me I better finish the quilt that night."

Donna stopped swinging and looked at me. "What would happen if you didn't finish that night?"

I swallowed hard, but said nothing.

Donna frowned. "Did she threaten you?" Her eyes widened. "Good Lord. She didn't threaten to shoot you, did she?"

I shook my head as my stomach tightened. It was worse.

"What are you two doing out here?" Agnes stepped out onto the porch with Petunia in tow. The goat let out a bleat and shook her head. "Easy now, Petunia. Here, have some food." Agnes pulled a Zip-lock bag out of her pocket and opened it. The goat stuck her face inside the bag and began chewing.

"Are those cookies?" I cocked my head.

"Peanut butter. They are her favorites." Agnes sighed. "I had to bring her outside because she kept jumping up in Elizabeth's lap so she could eat the pound cake Weenie made."

I narrowed my eyes. "Does Petunia belong to Elizabeth?"

"Oh no. She belongs to Heather, who works for Elizabeth. Heather's boyfriend, Grayson, gave her the little goat as a makeup present when they were arguing."

I crossed my arms. "I think I would have preferred flowers to a goat."

Donna chuckled. "Petunia is quite friendly. And you'll definitely be seeing more of her. She comes to all our quilting bees that we have at your mom's store."

"Really?"

"Yes, Heather helps run Elizabeth's flower farm and Petunia can't seem to stop eating up the flowers. So Elizabeth babysits her." Agnes smiled.

"She babysits a goat?"

"Sure does." Agnes rubbed the goat between the ears.

"Donna, can you come inside?" Elizabeth's voice called out from inside the house. "We have a question for you? About what kind of fertilizer you use on your prize-winning tomatoes."

Donna rolled her eyes and stood. "Excuse me, ladies." She pulled her cooler inside and shut the door behind her.

Petunia wandered over to me.

"Is she friendly?" I looked at Agnes.

"Sure is. But don't bother her when she's eating. She gets kind of ornery." Agnes gave her a look.

"That's understandable. I don't enjoy being interrupted when I'm eating a pint of Rocky Road." Right now, I could use a gallon.

"I didn't see your car in the driveway." Agnes shielded her eyes with her hand as she looked past me.

"Mom was too upset to drive, so I drove her car. I hope to get it this afternoon, once the police settle everything. Then it will be back to business."

"Mildred would hate that I'm telling you this, but…"

I stopped swinging and looked at her. "Tell me what?"

Agnes pressed her lips into a thin line for a fraction of a second. "Your mom's had a hard go the last few years with her quilt shop. She thought she would have to close up shop. Now that there's been a murder, a lot of people are not going to want to do business there."

"She never said anything about closing." My stomach rolled.

Agnes sighed heavily. "There's not a demand for homemade quilts. People aren't as sentimental as they used to be. Besides, if they want a quilt, they'll just buy it online."

"But those aren't original quilts. They're not even sewed on a long arm machine. They are mass-produced."

Agnes held up her hands. "Look, I get it. People these days want fast and easy. They don't care about quality."

I sighed. "I know she's got a lot of orders for longarm quilting. Half of the orders wanted detailed quilting, which she charges more for. Once the quilt shop opens, I'll get started on those right away. In the meantime, I wonder if she'd let me do some advertising to draw in more business."

Agnes gave a little smile. "I don't know, but I think that sounds like a great idea. Let me know what ideas you have, and I'll be glad to help. Heck, the entire quilting group will help."

For the first time that day, my heart felt a little light. "That would be great."

"I'm taking Petunia inside. Come on in when you're ready." Agnes guided the goat inside through the front door.

I stood and spotted the tow truck turning the corner onto the street in front of the house. It was pulling my car behind it.

I ran down the steps and yelled to the driver to stop. I ran down the sidewalk a few yards before the tow truck stopped.

"What's with all the screaming? Did I hit a dog or something?" The driver squinted at me through the passenger's side window. He was wearing a gray short-sleeved shirt with a patch on the pocket, which read Jerry and grease stained jeans.

"Why are you towing my car? I didn't violate any parking rules." I glared at him.

"Your car?" His eyes widened.

"Yes, my car. At Mildred's Quilt Shop. I'm her

daughter and work there. I demand you give me back my car."

"I can't do that."

"Why not?" I curled my fingers into fists at my side.

"Because the police have impounded this car as part of the crime scene. You're their number one suspect." He locked the truck and rolled up the window.

He drove away with me standing in the middle of Elm Street, staring after my car, completely stunned.

A couple of neighbors who had probably heard screaming came out of their houses and stood gawking at me.

I felt my face heat with anger and frustration at the possibility of the whole town thinking I was a murderer.

CHAPTER 4

"You can open the shop back up on Monday."

When Dean spoke those eight words, I wanted to cry with relief.

"Perfect. I'll be there bright and early." I had a ton of quilts to finish to help get my mom's business back on track. "Hey, when am I going to get my car back?"

"You'll get your car back when the police department is finished combing it for evidence." Dean's voice was harsh through the phone.

"How do you expect me to get around town?" My tone was less than friendly.

"Don't be so dramatic. Use your mom's car."

I curled my fingers into fists at his attitude.

"There's something else. You'll need to be at the quilt shop before Monday."

"Why is that?"

"You're going to need to clean up the murder area."

I gagged a little. "What? Me?"

"Yes, you. The police department isn't responsible for cleaning up the crime scene."

"But there's …" I gagged, trying to say the words.

"Blood. There's blood, Dove."

I shivered. "Yes. So, what do I do? Is there somebody I can call?"

"There is a company out of Jackson that cleans up crime scenes. But I have to warn you, it's expensive."

"How expensive?"

"It starts at a thousand dollars and goes up," Dean stated. "I have the number if you want it."

"Never mind." I had the urge to tell him exactly where he could put his number, but I restrained myself.

"If you don't pay someone to clean it, then you'll have to clean it yourself."

"We took biology together. Remember? I don't do well with blood." The image of dissecting a pig in class rose in my mind. I didn't have the heart to hack into the dead animal, and I had a tendency to pass out at first sight of blood.

Dean chuckled. "Yes. Well, we all change."

The phone went dead.

I walked into the living room. Mom had fallen asleep in her recliner, the unfinished quilt she'd been working on across her lap.

I carefully removed the quilt and placed it on the couch. She'd been appliqueing animals to the Noah's Arc baby quilt she was doing for a client's grandchild. The baby was due at the end of the month, and Mom had promised she would be finished long before then.

I grabbed the log cabin quilt from the back of the couch and draped it over Mom. She stirred but went right back to sleep.

I slipped into the kitchen and looked out into the backyard. Mom had lined the privacy fence with flower beds, and roses of every color were in full bloom.

I might not like the heat in Mississippi, but I adored the roses that seemed to flourish.

I took my cell phone out of my jeans pocket and went through my contact list. When I left Harland Creek, I'd not kept in contact with my friends from high school. Not that I had that many close friends. I'd been so head over heels in love with Dean in high school, I'd spent every waking hour with him.

Until we broke up.

The house phone rang, and I sprang over to answer it before it could ring a second time.

"Hello?" I kept my voice low and quiet.

"Dove? Is that you? I can barely hear you." The older woman screeched.

I tried but couldn't place which of Mom's friends I was talking to.

"Mom fell asleep in the recliner, and I'm trying not to wake her up," I whispered.

"Yes, your poor mother. I can't imagine what she's going through. I was just calling to let you know I'm bringing over one of my famous pound cakes for you and your mom."

I jolted upright. I knew immediately I was speaking to Bertha Mills.

"Oh please, don't do that!" The woman was famous for her hard-as-a-rock cakes and suspicious-tasting tuna casseroles. Whenever there was a dinner at church, the Harland Creek ladies always flagged Bertha's food so some unsuspecting fool wouldn't eat it.

"Why not?" Bertha growled on the other end of the line.

"Because I'm just about to leave. I have to clean up the quilt shop to get it ready to open on Monday."

"I see. Need any help?" Bertha offered.

"Actually, yes. Thank you." When it came to cleaning up a crime scene, I wasn't about to reject any offer of help. Bertha was a lot older than me and could handle the sight of blood better than I could.

"I'll see you over there in about fifteen minutes." I ended the call.

I gathered some Clorox, a mop, paper towels, a roll of garbage bags, and some deodorizer. Mom kept a mask for when she cut the grass, but I couldn't find it. I retrieved an old red bandana from my dresser drawer and stuck it in my bag of goodies. Since my car was still impounded, I grabbed Mom's car keys and scribbled a quick note to let her know where I was.

I quickly put all my items in the trunk of the car and got into the driver's seat. Within a few minutes, I was pulling up to the front of the quilt shop.

When I killed the engine, I was pleasantly surprised

that there was no backfire or smoke rising from the tailpipe, like my car.

I grabbed the keys before popping the trunk.

As soon as I climbed out of the car, the humidity slapped me in the face.

I had found another of Mom's ridiculous T-shirts to wear. Today's ensemble was a white T-shirt with a cow wearing a bow in her hair. It was captioned with the words, "Not today, heifer." I wore some denim shorts from high school I had found in my dresser. Mom never threw anything away.

If I were staying in Harland Creek for a while, I was going to need to buy some casual clothes without words or animals across the front. I had filled my suitcase with the few designer clothes I had left in my possession, but they were too dressy for every day.

I set my bucket filled with the cleaning items by the front door and leaned the mop against the window. I pulled out the keys to unlock the door.

I opened the door, carefully stepping inside with the items in my hand. "Hello?" I'm not sure why I called out, other than to make sure the ghost of Gertrude Brown had crossed to the other side and wasn't still trapped among the bolts of fabric and spools of thread.

Silence greeted me.

I relaxed a little and flipped the light switch. The room was flooded with light. The front of the store looked like a regular quilt shop, like nothing scary would ever happen in here.

A loud bleat had me jumping straight in the air. The

MYSTERY OF THE TEA CUP QUILT

bucket and mop fell to the floor in a clatter. I spun around. Bertha, Weenie, and the goat named Petunia stood in the doorway.

"Sorry. I didn't mean to frighten you." Weenie gave me a shy smile. Weenie was the quiet one out of the quilting crowd. She wore faded denim jeans and a black shirt with an apron on top.

"I brought Weenie along to help," Bertha nodded.

"What about Petunia?" I looked at the goat, who had locked eyes on a colorful bolt of Kaffe Fassett fabric.

"I was babysitting her for Elizabeth. I couldn't leave her alone, so I brought her. I told Agnes, and she's coming to pick her up." Weenie ducked her head.

Petunia strained against the leash to reach the colorful fabric with her lips.

"Where's the crime scene?" Bertha lifted her chin.

"In the back room. This way." I led the way to the room where Gertrude had been found.

I reached for the light, squeezed my eyes shut, and flipped the switch.

"Huh," Bertha grunted.

"Oh," Weenie whispered.

"What is it? Is it bad?" My hand tightened around the handle of the bucket.

"Well, it's not good." Agnes's voice had me turning around.

"Agnes, what are you doing here?"

She narrowed her eyes at Bertha. "Because I'm looking for her. Bertha, did you know your cows are out in my pasture again?"

Bertha glanced away. "No."

Agnes glared. "Well, they are. A cow knocked over one of my beehives. It took me half the morning to get it set back up, and all the bees calmed down."

"Fine. I'll go get them back in the pasture, but I'm going to need help." Bertha groused.

"I would say call Winston to help you. He'll do anything for a dollar. But since his aunt's death is pretty fresh, call Grayson."

Bertha let out a heavy sigh. "Fine." She cut her eyes at me. "Good luck."

Agnes waited until Bertha was out the door before turning back to me. "You realize Bertha wasn't planning on helping at all. She is just nosy, and wanted to see where Gertrude got whacked."

"Whacked?"

"Yeah. Whacked. That's what they say in those gangster movies." Agnes looked pretty pleased with herself for throwing around some new lingo.

I looked up at the ceiling. "Is there a lot of blood?"

Agnes snorted. "Haven't you looked at the floor yet?"

"No, the sight of blood makes me … queasy," I admitted. The coppery scent of the blood was just now reaching me. I tried to think of happy thoughts.

Agnes let out a laugh. "I think that alone should clear you as the murderer. Come on Weenie. Let Dove hold Petunia's leash and we'll get the floor cleaned up."

"Thank you." I walked out of the room with Petunia,

while Agnes and Weenie got busy cleaning up the crime scene.

Petunia spotted a quilt on the wall with appliqued flowers and walked over there.

"It's not real flowers," I told her and leaned against the wall. "Thank you guys for doing this. I know it's a big favor, but I appreciate it," I called out.

Weenie poked her head out of the room. "Are you kidding? This is more exciting than watching Perry Mason in the evenings." She grinned and then disappeared back into the room.

"I've never seen a real-life crime scene before. Much more blood than I expected." Agnes called out.

My stomach rolled, as I slid down the wall. I felt a tug on the leash and looked over at Petunia. She was gnawing on the edge of the quilt hanging on the wall. I crawled over and pulled her back.

"Stop that!"

She narrowed her goat eyes at me and let out a bleat.

"Everything okay out there?" Agnes asked.

"Petunia is trying to eat a quilt."

"She'll eat anything. Keep a sharp eye on her." Agnes chuckled.

Petunia reached over and began chewing on my hair.

"Eww. Stop that." I pulled out of her reach. "Come on. There are some leftover snacks in the back." I stood and led the goat where we kept the coffee pot. I tied her rope to the handle on a cabinet and opened the plastic container of snacks that Elizabeth had dropped off. When I held out a sweet treat, she gobbled it up.

Since we had to leave the quilt shop so fast after the murder, no one had time to clean the coffeepot. I quickly dumped the old coffee down the sink and cleaned up the pot.

"We're done." Weenie appeared in the doorway. "Come have a look."

I untied Petunia's rope and followed Weenie back into the room.

I stepped inside and was pleasantly greeted with the scent of lavender.

"We cleaned everything with Clorox and then sprayed the air freshener. Have a look and make sure we got everything before we leave." Weenie cocked her head.

I knelt and glanced at the steel rack which held the client's quilts. I looked at each quilt on the bottom, ensuring there had been no blood stains. "I don't see anything." I cringed as I reached my hand underneath the rack where I couldn't see. My hand brushed against something. I pulled back my hand and noticed a white powder on my fingertip.

"Look, I found something." I held up my hand. "Looks like medicine."

"Could be cocaine." Agnes offered.

"In Harland Creek?" I frowned.

"You never know. I'll get a zip-lock bag out of the back and we'll scoop it up."

"But shouldn't I call Dean and let him know?"

"If he was any kind of police chief, he would have found it himself." Agnes scowled.

I looked at Weenie. She nodded her head in agreement with Agnes.

"Fine. Get the Zip-lock."

Agnes returned with a quart-size bag.

I reached my hand back under and my finger came across something hard this time. I pulled it back. It was part of a white pill.

"Look. I bet this pill is part of that powder." I put the pill in the bag.

"I bet that belongs to the killer." Weenie offered. "I bet it's some kind of narcotic, and Gertrude was selling them. It could have been a drug deal gone wrong."

I frowned. "You see that on Perry Mason?"

"No. Matlock." Her eyes sparkled.

"You know she owned that RV campsite on the edge of town. I heard she was letting a lot of suspicious characters rent from her." Agnes cocked her head.

"This might sound mean and unchristian, but I'm glad she's gone." Weenie admitted.

Agnes and I looked at Weenie.

She wrung her hands together. "It's just that she did a lot of bad things to people. She always bailed her druggie nephew out of trouble. She cheated people and was a thief, and even ran a dogfighting ring before the police caught wind and she had the animals put down. If there was any way she could make a buck, Gertrude would do it. And the way she talked to poor Mildred..." Weenie shook her head. "I have to admit something. I kept praying for God to take her away. " She gave us a strained look. "You don't think this is my fault, do you? You don't think God took her because I prayed for it?"

I stood and placed my hands on her shoulders. "Weenie, I don't think God works that way."

She gave me a grateful smile.

I frowned when I heard footsteps. I looked over at Agnes. "Are you expecting anyone?"

She shook her head.

I stuck my Zip-lock bag in my pocket, grabbed Petunia's leash, and walked toward the front of the store.

A man in his late twenties was standing over the cash register. Despite the heat, he was wearing a black hoodie and baggy jeans.

"We're not open." I stated. Agnes appeared at my elbow and I was grateful for the support.

He glared at me. His face was skeletal and his eyes, dark and sunken into pale skin. He shoved his hoodie back and snarled, his discolored teeth looking more like an animal than human.

"You. You're Dove." He raised a bony hand and pointed in my direction. "You murdered my Aunt Gertrude."

His words had knocked the wind out of me, and it took a few seconds for me to respond to his ludicrous accusation.

"I did not."

He shook his head. "That's not what the cops said.

They found her here, and you were the last to see her alive."

"Well, the cops are wrong." I stated. Petunia let out a bleat in support of my innocence.

He looked down and frowned when he spotted Petunia. "That's a goat."

Agnes shoved past me. "Yes, and she's an attack goat. She's trained to attack. You better get out of here before you make her mad."

His eyes widened at her words, and he took a step back. Petunia bleated again, straining against her leash.

He shook his head but never took his eyes off the goat. "I heard you two arguing the night she died. You won't get away with this. You'll pay for what you did to Aunt Gertrude." He turned and sprinted out the door.

My stomach dropped. Had he heard Gertrude threaten me about my secret?

I cleared my throat. "So that's the nephew?" I looked at Weenie.

She nodded. "Yes, that's Winston. He's a loose cannon. If I were you, I would sleep with one eye open. He breaks into people's homes so he can get money for his drug habit."

"Perfect." I reached into my pocket and brushed against the Zip-lock bag.

"Dove, what were you and Gertrude arguing about at night? I thought you yelled at her while the shop was open?" Agnes frowned.

Guilt twisted my gut. Apparently she hadn't overheard my conversation with Dean. "I stayed late to finish some work. Gertrude dropped by after we closed. We were arguing about that stupid quilt." I lied.

"So, what are you going to do?" Weenie looked at me.

"I need to go find Dean. He needs to find the real killer before this town puts me on trial for something I didn't do."

CHAPTER 5

Upon returning home, I spotted a police car parked in front of the house. I tried to stay calm, but I was on edge after my run-in with Winston.

I climbed out of Mom's car and popped the trunk. Just as I was getting the mop and bucket out, the front door opened.

"Dove? Why didn't you wake me up? I would have helped clean up the store." She gave me a frown from the porch.

After shutting the trunk, I walked toward her. "You were sleeping so well. I didn't want to wake you."

She glanced at the mop in my hand and grimaced. "Did you do all that yourself? I know how you feel about blood."

I stepped inside, headed to the kitchen. "No. Bertha and Weenie met me over there, along with Petunia." I set the bucket on the floor and took the mop into the laundry room off the kitchen.

"Bertha helped?"

I laughed and stuck the mop in the trash can. I would have to buy her a new one. Even though it had been cleaned thoroughly with bleach, there was no way I could let Mom use something that had been used to clean up a crime scene. "No. Agnes showed up, and Bertha left to go get her cows. Agnes and Weenie did all the work. I need to repay them. Maybe bake them something." I walked back into the kitchen and stopped short when Dean appeared.

"Hello, Dove." His deep voice made my stomach warm. How could someone make me so mad yet make me want to kiss him?

I shook my head, dislodging my traitorous thoughts. "Hello, Dean."

"Dean came over to update me on the crime. We've already chatted, so he's going to catch you up. I need to run over to Sylvia's house. She forgot to pick up the fabric for our next quilt project." She gave my arm a reassuring squeeze and grabbed the keys to her car off the kitchen counter before scurrying out the front door.

I turned to busy myself with making a pot of coffee.

"You survived the cleanup, I see." His booted footsteps seemed to echo on the cream-colored linoleum floor.

I swallowed while grabbing two coffee mugs out of the cabinet. "Like I said, I didn't do any of it." I turned around. He stretched his lean figure into one of the kitchen chairs. He wasn't wearing his uniform, just jeans and a black T-shirt stretched to an inch of its life across the hard muscles of his chest.

I walked over and sat across from him in a chair while waiting for the coffee to brew. "So any updates on the case?"

"The coroner's report concluded that Gertrude died of blunt force trauma to the back of the head. Which meant the murderer hit her from behind."

"But we found her face up?"

"Yes." A slow grin played at his mouth. "Which meant the force that she was hit with spun her around and she fell backward onto the floor. We searched the shop for the murder weapon. It wasn't there."

I shivered and shoved my hand into my pocket. My finger brushed against the Zip-lock bag.

"What about blood work? Did they test for drugs in her system?" I cocked my head.

"Her system was clean, except for some alcohol detected in her blood. It wasn't enough for her to be intoxicated. Everyone knew Gertrude liked gin." He lost the grin and sat up in the chair, leaning toward me. "Why did you ask about drugs?"

"Because her nephew came into the shop while we … while Agnes and Weenie were cleaning."

He leaned forward in the chair and narrowed his eyes. "Winston? What did he say?"

"He accused me of murdering his aunt. He said the cops told him I was the one who did it." I glared.

Dean let out a curse and stood abruptly. He shoved his hand through his dark hair. "That's not what I said.

He must have overheard some cops talking about impounding your car for evidence."

"Now that you bring it up." I stood and walked back to the coffee pot. "When can I get my car back?"

"I'll bring it over later today."

I sighed heavily. "You realize, half the town thinks I murdered that old woman."

"Dove, that's not true."

I spun around, glaring at him. "Do *you* think I did it?"

He stared at me for a long time before finally answering. "As police chief, I am not allowed to give my opinion. I can only look at the facts. The facts are, you had an argument which was witnessed by several customers. You were also the last person to see her alive that night."

"Not true. The murderer was the last person to see Gertrude alive." I poured myself a cup of coffee and then poured Dean one. I shoved the cup at him before taking my seat at the kitchen table.

He sighed heavily. "There is only one door leading into the quilt shop. The only people who have keys are you and your mom."

"That means nothing. Someone could have stolen a key." I lifted my chin.

He studied me before taking a sip of coffee. "Possibly."

"Well, I think you need to look into Winston. He gives me the creeps. Not to mention he said he was at the quilt shop that night. He said he overheard me and Gertrude."

"Really? He didn't mention that to us. He gave us an alibi that he wasn't even in town. We are checking it out. I don't want you to engage with him again. If you see him, run the other way and call me."

"What if he breaks in here?" My eyes grew wide.

"I can have an officer increase his patrol rounds on this street."

"Maybe I need a gun," I muttered to myself.

"I would highly suggest you don't. You don't need to be in possession of a deadly weapon." He glared.

I lifted my chin. "Fine. Then I'll get a dog."

"You don't like dogs." He deadpanned.

I cringed. "They don't like me. In the meantime, promise me you'll check out Winston."

He nodded. "I will."

"Surely you have other leads you are looking into."

"A few. Someone reported she got into a verbal argument with one of tenants in that RV park she owned. And of course, we are looking into Louie."

"Who's Louie?"

"He's the guy who collects all her rent on her rental properties. I get the distinct sense he's had run-ins with the law before, but I ran a report on him, nothing came up. It's almost like he doesn't exist."

She sighed.

"Don't leave town." His gaze drifted down to my T-shirt. "You really need to stop wearing your mom's T-shirts." He left the kitchen and walked out the front door.

After the door closed, I pulled out the Zip-lock bag and looked at the partial pill.

Maybe I should have told Dean about my discovery. But I couldn't help but feel like he would discount my find.

I decided to hang onto the pill and maybe do a little digging on my own.

CHAPTER 6

I got up early Monday morning to get to the quilt shop a few hours before it opened, hoping to get a start on some of the quilting orders. I'd had two cups of coffee and wore a respectable T-shirt with a large sunflower on the front.

Dean was as good as his word. When I looked outside, my car was sitting in my driveway, as promised.

I was determined that today would be a good day.

After turning on the lights and the longarm quilting machine, I walked to the room where we kept the unfinished and finished quilts.

I stepped inside, glancing down at the floor where Gertrude had been found.

I shook my head, shoved back those terrible images, and walked over to the shelf.

Glancing at the calendar, I saw that Nettie Halston's sampler quilt was next on the list to be quilted. I searched through the quilts to find hers. I stopped when I spotted Gertrude's Tea Cup Quilt.

Now that she was gone, I wondered if I should call Winston to come pick it up. I cringed. He would probably just try to sell it at the local pawnshop to get money to buy drugs.

As far as I knew, Gertrude had no other living relatives.

I would talk it over with Mom and let her make the final decision on what to do with the quilt.

In the meantime, I decided to put the quilt in Mom's office so it would be out of the way.

I then picked up Nettie's colorful quilt top, made with fabric by Bonnie and Camille. I was glad to see that Nettie had requested the quilt be stippled and not detailed. I knew I could get this quilt done fairly quickly and move onto the next order.

After I loaded the quilt top, batting and the backing into the longarm, I began quilting.

As I guided the needle around in a meandering pattern, I let my mind wander over who the murderer could be.

Winston was at the top of my list. I knew from watching crime shows, people were generally murdered by someone they knew.

Winston was Gertrude's nephew and a drug addict. Maybe he killed her in a fit of rage when he needed drug money and she refused to give him any?

I frowned as I recalled Weenie saying Gertrude had

done bad things to a lot of people in Harland Creek. Maybe I shouldn't rule anyone out?

By the time Mom and Patricia arrived at the shop, I was making good progress on the quilt.

Mom popped into the room, smiling as she examined the quilt. "That looks lovely, Dove. I'm glad Nettie didn't want to have it detailed. This style looks so much better with the blocks."

"I agree." When I came to the edge of the quilt, I stopped. I looked over Mom's shoulder at Patricia, standing there with her inhaler in her hand.

"Good morning, Patricia." I gave her a friendly smile.

She looked at me with uncertainty in her eyes. "Good morning." She put her inhaler to her lips and took a pull. "I need to get back out front." She turned and hurried away.

I frowned at Mom. "Is she always that nervous?"

Mom rolled her eyes. "She's always been jittery, but since the murder happened, she's worse. I caught her rubbing a rabbit's foot she carries on her keychain before she walked in the front door. And now she's hung up a necklace with an evil eye over the register."

"That's being dramatic, don't you think?"

"Yes, but I don't want to hurt her feelings." She held up the pink quilt in her hand. "I need to get started on the binding of this baby quilt. Let me know if you need me." She squeezed my shoulder and left the room.

I started back quilting. Before I realized it, it was almost noon.

"Can you come out here, Dove?" Mom poked her head in the room. "It seems we have an influx of customers." She looked at the quilt I was working on. "Wow, are you done already?"

"Yes. All it needs is the binding."

Her face lit up. "I can finish that today. Nettie should have it by tomorrow. Good job, sweetie. We may turn the business around yet."

I started taking the quilt out of the frame. "Mom, I wanted to talk to you about that…"

Mom's eyes revealed she slipped up. "Not now, Dove. We need to take care of the customers first."

I stopped what I was doing and headed into the front of the shop.

I was shocked to see how many people there were. Patricia was calculating and cutting some fabric from a bolt while others lined up behind her. A few women were taking photos of the store with their phones.

There was one man who stood out among the crowd. He was tall and broad and looked like he was a retired linebacker for the NFL. He wore a black long-sleeve button-up shirt and black jeans with expensive cowboy boots. His salt and pepper hair was slicked back, and he leaned against the wall with a toothpick hanging out of the corner of his mouth.

His dark beady eyes roamed over the store before his intense scrutiny landed on me. He narrowed his gaze as if I were his target.

I sidled up to Patricia. "Patricia, who's that man over there?"

Her anxious eyes grew wide. "That's Louie. Gertrude's…employee."

"What's he want?"

She shook her head, reached over and grabbed the evil eye necklace and rubbed it like a genie's lamp. "I don't know, and I don't want to find out. They say he has a criminal past. Whenever Gertrude wanted someone to comply with what she wanted, she would send Louie."

"So, why don't the police do anything about him?" I narrowed my gaze right back on Louie. I wanted him to know I would not be intimidated.

"Because everyone is scared of him. Now that Gertrude is gone, rumor is he will inherit everything."

I jerked my head back to her. "Louie? What about Winston?"

"There's talk that Gertrude and Winston got into a big argument in the parking lot of Mac's Grocery. She was telling him she would cut him out of her will and he would never get a penny out of her again?"

"Winston must have done something to make her mad enough to cut him from her will."

Patricia shrugged. "I don't know. I have to get back to work." She turned her attention back to the older woman wanting two yards of a Moda fabric.

I looked at Mom and saw the worry etched on her face.

I needed to get Louie out of the shop before he caused a scene.

Squaring my shoulders and lifting my chin, I marched straight over to him.

"You must be Louie."

He frowned and straightened when I approached. He seemed a little taken aback by my boldness. "You must be Dove. The one who found Gertrude."

I didn't bother telling him Elizabeth and Mom were with me when the body was discovered.

"Yes. You worked for Gertrude?"

"I did." He narrowed his eyes.

"I am sorry for your loss. Please accept my condolences."

"Your what?" He snarled and then shook his head. "I don't want any of your condolences. I'm just here to pick up the quilt Gertrude made."

I blinked. I wasn't expecting that.

"Do you usually pick up her quilting?"

"I do whatever she asks. She told me if she hadn't gotten her quilt by Thursday, to come by Friday and pick it up. But the shop was closed, because she was murdered here."

I screwed up my courage. "Did whatever Gertrude wanted? What if she asked you to do something criminal? Would you do it?"

He propped his hands on his hips. "Everybody has to earn a living."

His frankness startled and frightened me. "Did you see Gertrude on the night she died?"

"Yes. She cooked dinner for me."

"What time was this?"

"Six o'clock. She liked to eat early."

"So you didn't see her after?"

"Nope."

"What were you doing between the time of midnight and four o'clock?"

A slow smile crossed his lips, and he leaned toward me. "None of your damn business. Now give me the quilt."

"I would love to, but the police took it into evidence." She shrugged.

His eyes narrowed. "They what? What do they want with a quilt?"

"I don't know. You'll have to ask them. Talk to Dean. I'm sure he can help you." I knew from the look on his face, he wouldn't go near the police station to talk to Dean.

He shoved off the wall and stormed out the front door.

"Dove, are you okay?" Maggie and Sylvia, two of the quilters, appeared on either side of me.

"I'm okay. That guy gives me the creeps."

"No doubt. He's as low as a snake." Maggie narrowed her eyes. "I wouldn't put it past him to kill Gertrude. Especially if he knew he would get everything in her will."

I looked at Maggie. "So you heard that, too?"

She nodded.

"He doesn't have an alibi for the time when Gertrude was murdered. And I'm sure he could have picked the lock."

"Weenie said she came home to find Louie standing in her kitchen and eating her homemade apple pie. She was so scared that she didn't know what to do." Sylvia shook her head.

"Did she call the cops?"

"No. She was too scared that he would hurt her if she did. She said he ate her pie and then left. She had the locks changed after that." Sylvia sighed. "I don't think locks will keep a man like Louie out."

I went to the front door and saw Louie climb into a black Dodge Charger. The engine roared to life, and he spun tires out of the parking lot.

This just got interesting. One more suspect to add to my list.

CHAPTER 7

"I really don't want to go." I cut my eyes at Mom from my comfy spot on the couch. It was Wednesday, and I had gone to the quilt shop early each morning to start quilting. So far I had finished two queen-size quilts and was almost finished detailing a lap-size quilt. I was tired. All I wanted was to eat something comforting and veg out on the couch.

"As long as you are staying in this house, Dove, you'll go to church with me." Mom gave me a look that let me know she was serious.

"I'll go on Sunday. Besides, I'm starving. I missed lunch."

"You're in luck. It's potluck Wednesday." She tugged off her apron and walked into the kitchen.

"Potluck?" I followed her, my interest and stomach now piqued.

Mom pulled down her insulated casserole carrier from the pantry and looked at me. "Yes. Pastor John started having potluck the first Wednesday of the month to encourage more people to attend." Sticking her hands into the potholders, she pulled the casserole out of the oven and placed it in the carrier. The heavenly aroma of the chicken casserole made my mouth water.

"What if people won't talk to me? Or worse, what if they talk to me about the murder?" I slumped into one of the kitchen chairs. Suddenly my appetite was gone.

Mom shook her head, walked over and eased into the chair beside me. "It's church, honey. The safest place you can go." She squeezed my arm and stood. "Besides, Elizabeth will be bringing homemade cinnamon rolls. I know they are your favorite."

I sat up straight. "Fine. You've worn me down. I'll go, but I'm not wearing a dress."

Fifteen minutes later, I was dressed in white jeans and a pretty yellow blouse. I wore my hair up in a braid, not to be fancy, but to help combat the humidity. My mom glanced at my expensive heels with the black bow on the back.

"Nice shoes. When I was young, I wore heels all the time. Now I choose comfort over fashion." She smiled, looped her purse strap on her arm, and picked up the casserole carrier. "Let's take my car. Keys are on the counter."

I grabbed the keys and then took the insulated carrier. After Mom was seated in the passenger's seat, I handed her the dish.

We arrived at First Baptist Church fifteen minutes

before it was time to eat. After I parked Mom quickly got out. Weenie pulled up beside us with Elizabeth and Agnes riding in the backseat. They all scrambled out.

"Good to see you, Dove." Weenie gave me a shy smile.

"Hi, Weenie. Are you taxiing around Elizabeth and Agnes?"

Weenie cut her eyes at her two friends then laughed nervously. "Figured we would save money on gas."

Sylvia and Maggie walked up. "You know that's a lie. They are riding together because they are doing some investigation on this murder case. And we want in. No way are y'all leaving us out." Sylvia pulled out a small cylinder pump from her purse. "This quilting sleuth group needs me. I'm the one with the mace. In case the killer is on to us, and we need protection."

I held up my hands. "There is no quilting sleuth group. Let the police do their job. I'm sure Dean is probably close to catching the killer. Besides, I don't want any of you ladies to put yourselves in danger."

They all gave me glares.

I needed backup. I turned around to Mom. "Please tell your friends that this isn't a good idea."

She stood there, holding her casserole, and averted her eyes. "Honey, it's not a bad idea to check out other leads. The police can't be everywhere."

"Mom! You knew about this?"

Agnes snorted. "It was your mom's idea."

My mouth dropped. "Mom…."

"Now, before you say anything, I just want you to

know that we're not doing anything illegal. We are just putting our heads together and throwing out ideas as to who the killer might be." She lifted her chin. "You have no idea how much information we have acquired over the years."

I blinked. I didn't know if I should be angry or grateful.

"Good evening, ladies," Pastor John greeted us warmly as he walked toward us. "Here, Mildred. Let me take that for you."

"Thank you, Pastor." Mom handed him the casserole carrier. "Dove and I will help Elizabeth and Agnes get their things."

"Perfect. I'll see everyone inside." Pastor John headed into the white church.

Mom's smile slid off her face as she looked at her group of friends. "No more talk about the murder for now. Tomorrow we will discuss theories when we meet for the quilting bee at the shop. Come on, Dove. Let's get the rest of this food inside." She walked over to Weenie's open trunk and picked up the dish of cinnamon rolls. "Take this, and I'll help with the other stuff."

"Mom…"

"Dove. Go." She gave me one of her looks, and I knew the conversation was over.

"Fine. But we are going to discuss this when we get home." I scowled and headed inside. I walked through the sanctuary to the back of the building where the fellowship hall was located. The church had recently renovated this part of the building, and I was pleasantly surprised to see how nice it looked. I set the plate of cinnamon rolls down on the end of the counter next to a coconut cake.

"You're the last person I expected to see walk through the church doors."

I cringed and turned at the sound of the familiar feminine voice.

"Hello, Eleanor." I forced a smile to her face. Eleanor Simmons was Pastor John's spinster sister. Their father had left a large inheritance to his children but he put Eleanor, the favorite child, in charge of doling out the money. While Pastor John was generous and kind, Eleanor was stingy and cruel. She had to be in her late sixties, but with all the Botox and fillers she stuck in her face, she could pass for forty.

"I'm surprised you had the nerve to show up here." Eleanor set her expensive purse down on the counter. She pointed her thin nose in the air and examined her hundred-dollar manicure. She wore an expensive black dress which was tailored to her slim figure and matching Louboutin shoes.

My stomach clenched with butterflies. As a child, she always intimidated me with a withering glare. As an adult, nothing had changed.

"Why would you say that, Eleanor?" I steeled my spine.

She gave an elegant snort. "After being accused of murder, I would have expected you to hide out in your mom's house, unable to show your face in town."

"I'm not sure where you got your facts, but they are wrong. I haven't been accused of anything."

Agnes walked into the fellowship hall and spotted us. She glared and made a beeline straight for us.

"Eleanor." She stepped in between us and set down a dish on the counter. "I see you are here for the food. Again. You only show up at church when we have food." Agnes cocked her head. "You're not going hungry, are you, honey?"

Eleanor glared at the older woman's insinuation. "I have other obligations that pull at my time. I have to spread myself thin to make sure Harland Creek remains an upstanding town." She cut her eyes at me. "Seems like that is becoming harder since Dove arrived in town.

Agnes gave the woman her full attention. "So I've been meaning to ask you about your last ladies' luncheon that you hosted. I heard that you threatened Gertrude when she crashed your party."

Eleanor's face went red. "That's not true. You know Gertrude. She was always trying to wiggle her way into my circle of influence. She might have had money, but that doesn't buy you respect or class.."

"Huh. Well, I heard you threatened her if she dared to show up at your house again." Agnes smirked. "Because if that is true, you would be a suspect."

"You better keep your nose out of my business, old woman." Eleanor snarled and snatched the purse off the counter. The handle caught on a candlestick, sending the bag's contents and the candlestick crashing to the ground.

"Look what you made me do." Eleanor glared at Agnes before bending to the ground to gather her items.

"Can't stay and chat. Have to help get the rest of the food inside." Agnes gave me a wink and disappeared out into the sanctuary.

I bent and gathered a tube of red lipstick, a package of gum, and a cigarette lighter. "Here," I handed the items to Elanor.

"Give me those." She stuffed the items into her purse. She stood, hiked her purse on her boney shoulder, and exited the back door.

"Rude woman." I shook my head, gathered the candlestick, and set it on the table. The candle rolled halfway under a table in the corner. I bent, lifted the tablecloth and grabbed the candle.

I spotted something else.

"Dove, what are you doing?" Mom asked as she entered the room.

My hand reached out and grabbed the item. Standing up, I held what appeared to be a small leather-zipped pouch.

"This must have fallen out of Eleanor's purse. Looks like a manicure set." I frowned and unzipped it.

I froze.

Mom walked into the room and met my gaze. "What is it?"

I turned the unzipped bag towards her. "It's a lock-picking kit."

Mom didn't say a word. Her expression said it all.

I cleared my throat and looked at her.

"Looks like you need to get your quilting group over to the shop tomorrow. I'm adding Eleanor Simmons to the list of suspects."

CHAPTER 8

"Dean, you need to look into this." I parked my hands on my hips and glared.

I had gotten to the police department early that morning, so I could talk to him. I decided last night to show him the evidence I'd found.

"Eleanor has a lot of commercial properties. She probably uses that lock-picking tool to get into her own buildings. It's not like she's going around town breaking and entering people's homes."

I arched an eyebrow. "What about people's shops? Have you considered that's how the murderer got into the quilt shop to kill Gertrude? They picked the lock?"

He gave me a stony look. I always hated that look. When we were dating, it was hard to tell what the man was thinking.

"Fine. If you don't want to talk about that, then let's discuss the other evidence I found. What about this?" I pulled out the Zip-lock bag with the partial pill inside.

"I discovered this underneath the shelf where Gertrude's body was found."

He snatched it out of my hand. "Dove, do you understand withholding evidence is a crime?" His eyes blazed.

"Well, your guys should have done a better job searching for evidence," I snarled.

"Dove, you need to go to work and let the police do what they do best."

I opened my mouth to give him a smart remark, but then slammed my lips shut.

I knew Dean. There was no use in arguing with him.

"Fine." I turned on my heel and headed for the door.

He grabbed my elbow. "Wait. Give me Eleanor's property so I can return it to her."

I groaned as I plucked it out of my purse and held it out. "Here."

He took it. "Just stay out of my way, okay?"

I glared, but said nothing. I stomped out of the police station and headed for my car.

When I finally pulled up to the quilt shop, I noticed five extra cars that were not normally there. I got out of my car and went to the door. The sign still said Closed, but the door was not locked.

My mom spun around the second I stepped foot into the quilt shop. "Finally, you are here. Let's go into the back room to get set up."

Elizabeth, Agnes, Weenie, Sylvia, Donna, Lorraine and even Bertha were there.

So they had actually shown up to discuss the murder. I was impressed.

"Aren't we missing someone?" I asked.

"Maggie had to work at the beauty shop." Sylvia nodded. "Cybil had a hair emergency. She tried coloring her hair at home to save a buck and turned the dang thing orange. Poor thing looks like Bozo, the clown. Maggie's trying to work her magic and fix it. I told her I would fill her in on everything when I got back."

"I'll lock the door since we're not supposed to be open for another hour." I flipped the lock and followed the ladies to the large room in the back, where Mom taught her weekly class for new quilt blocks. There were chairs set up in rows facing the counter with Mom's Bernina sewing machine. She also had a whiteboard where she would make notes. After she would show certain blocks, the ladies would go home and work on them. She always took the chairs out on Thursdays to make room for the quilting bee ladies and the quilt they would be hand quilting.

Lorraine stopped in front of the quilt block on the wall. "Mildred, are we ever going to do the Drunkards Path quilt? We've been talking about it for a while."

Mom nodded patiently. "Yes, I'm just trying to decide on the variation. Now, if everyone will take a seat, we can get started."

I watched as all the ladies sat down in the front row. Elizabeth and Agnes had their heads together, chatting. Lorraine and Donna both had pulled out a notebook and pens. Sylvia slipped her glasses on and stared straight ahead. Bertha and Weenie were the only ones who didn't get a seat upfront. They had to sit in the second row. Bertha mumbled something under her breath, while Weenie pulled out her yarn along with the needles, and began knitting while waiting for my mom to speak.

Mom looked at me. "Dove, would you like to say something first?"

Swallowing hard, I walked to the front of the room. "I know last night I wasn't too keen on any of us getting involved in investigating this murder. Something happened to change my mind."

"What happened?" Lorraine frowned.

"Two things." I looked at the ladies and I knew I had captured their attention. "First, Agnes let it slip in front of Eleanor that she knew Eleanor had threatened Gertrude when she crashed her ladies' luncheon."

Lorraine nodded. "I was there. I heard it myself."

"Woman, what have I told you about socializing with Eleanor?" Agnes shook her head.

"I wasn't socializing." Lorraine shrugged. "Eleanor invited me because I used to be Dr. Evan's nurse. Eleanor was always friendly with Dr. Evans, so I assume that's why I received an invitation. I was curious so I went. Plus I heard there would be mimosas. I've never had a mimosa."

"Dove, go ahead." Mom urged.

I licked my lips. "Second, after Eleanor spilled the contents of her purse, something fell out."

Weenie leaned forward as her knitting needles clicked together. "Was it a knife?"

"No…"

"Was it a gun?" Bertha offered.

"No…"

"Was it …" Agnes asked, but my mom quickly cut her off.

"If everyone can stop asking questions, Dove can tell you what she found." Mom glared.

The room went silent.

"I found a lock-picking kit."

Gasps went up around the room.

Agnes stood up with her finger in the air. "I knew it. That old bat killed Gertrude."

Elizabeth shook her head. "Let's not get ahead of ourselves. Dove, did you tell Dean about this?"

I narrowed my eyes. "Yes, I went by the police station this morning and told him. He dismissed it. He said Eleanor had many business properties and she probably needed it to get in on the rare occasion the renters had changed the locks."

"Bull crap." Agnes cursed.

Donna shot her a disapproving look.

I bit my lip to keep from laughing.

"Let's start with a list of suspects." Weenie smiled as her knitting needles clacked a mile a minute.

"Good idea, Weenie." I nodded and grabbed the dry-erase marker. "Number one suspect is…"

"You." Bertha blurted out.

I slowly turned.

"Well, she's not wrong, Dove." Sylvia gave me a pained smile. "Just put your name down and we can cross it off as soon as possible."

I groaned. "Fine." I wrote my name under number one. "Winston is also a suspect. He's her nephew, who has a drug habit. Remember we found that pill at the crime scene."

Agnes perked up. "We should have the pharmacist tell us what kind of medication it is. I bet it's oxycodone."

My shoulders slumped. "We can't. I turned that into Dean, too."

"Winston is my number one suspect. He's been known to break into people's homes. Maybe he used a lock-picking tool like Eleanor has to break into my quilt shop." Mom cocked her head as if she were considering the possibility. "I wish I had installed cameras a year ago when they had them on sale."

"Yeah, but it wouldn't be as much fun solving a case." Donna smiled and looked at me.

"Louie is a suspect." Sylvia nodded. "I was here when he threatened you, Dove. He worked for Gertrude, breaks into people's homes, and is as shady as they come."

I nodded and added Louie to the list.

"Eleanor is a suspect. I'm not sure she would actually kill Gertrude." Bertha stated. "She doesn't like to get her hands dirty. But she could have paid someone to do it."

"Right." I wrote Eleanor's name down.

MYSTERY OF THE TEA CUP QUILT

"I think we need to investigate Gertrude's house for clues. I noticed the police cars stationed at her home are now gone." Weenie smiled sweetly.

"We can't go now. We need to wait until it gets dark." Agnes looked around the room.

"What if we get in trouble?" Donna looked a bit concerned.

I smiled. Donna was a rule follower from the get-go.

"I'll be the one that is going into her house. I don't want any of you to get in trouble." I looked at all of them.

"If you're going. I'm going." Mom lifted her chin.

"Yeah, we're all going." Elizabeth nodded. All the ladies nodded, agreeing in unison.

I looked at my mom to control her friends.

She gave me a grin. "Looks like the quilting group has gone rogue. No use arguing, Dove."

I blew out a breath. I knew when I was beaten.

"Fine. Meet at Mom's house at ten."

I think we should leave our suspect list up, but rename them quilt blocks in case anyone sees this." Weenie didn't miss a beat with her knitting.

I blinked. "That's actually a good idea."

Weenie smiled.

Mom took the dry erase marker and began writing. "Dove is now Dove in the Window. Eleanor will be…

"Drunkards Path," Bertha snickered.

Everyone laughed. Eleanor had gotten a DUI

months ago and tried her best to hide it. But nothing was a secret in Harland Creek.

"What about Winston?" I asked.

"Courthouse Steps?" Donna suggested. "If he doesn't straighten up, he's going to be seeing a lot of courthouse steps."

Mom wrote down the block.

'What about Louie?" I looked around.

"Monkey Wrench?" Agnes spoke up.

Mom nodded and wrote the block name down. She stepped back after making sure the names were erased, leaving only the quilt block names in its place.

I bit my lip and hoped I wasn't making a huge mistake that could get someone hurt.

CHAPTER 9

I glanced at my reflection in the mirror. I'd braided my hair and slipped on a black trucker hat. I'd chosen a pair of black jeans and the only black T-shirt of Mom's, which had a gray cat holding a white bone in its mouth with the words, "I find this humerus," spattered across the chest.

I decided that beggars could not be choosers when it came to breaking and entering. The T-shirt would have to do.

I walked into the kitchen where all the ladies were sitting around the table drinking hot tea and passing tea cakes to one another. They had even brought Petunia, the goat, who was nibbling on a cookie off Elizabeth's plate.

I frowned. "What's going on here?"

Weenie looked up at me with a big smile and two black smudges under her eyes. She looked very much like a skinny raccoon. "Just getting our energy up before we go investigate the dead woman's house."

"Elizabeth, pass me a slice of that pound cake. I need to get my sugar up before we head out." Agnes held out her plate and Elizabeth placed a slice of cake on it.

Bertha looked over at me with a glare. "So what's the plan, genius?"

I let her snide comment roll off my back and studied the ladies. "Not everyone can come. I looked at Gertrude's house on google maps. Because she lives out in the country, there are no street lights, so it's going to be really dark. I don't want one of you to fall and break a hip."

Agnes pointed at Elizabeth. "That means Elizabeth is out. You've had your hip replaced once. The last thing you need is to trip and have to get the other one done."

Elizabeth snorted. "If we are going by who's a fall risk, then Lorraine is out, too." She looked at me. "Lorraine had her knee replaced last summer."

I felt a headache mounting. I looked around the room. "Everyone who has had a hip replacement or knee replacement, raise your hand."

Elizabeth and Lorraine raised their hands.

"What about if they need a knee replacement?" Donna asked.

I blew out a breath. "Raise your hand if you need a knee replacement."

Sylvia raised her hand.

Agnes snorted. "You'd be better off asking who doesn't have health issues. The last thing you need is someone getting stressed out and falling out because of low blood sugar or having a heart attack in a house they've broken into."

I groaned. "Agnes is right. Raise your hand if you have health issues."

"Honey, we are in our sixties and seventies. We all have health issues." Maggie snorted.

"I wore my new sneakers in case we have to make a quick getaway." Weenie stuck out her feet so we could all admire her shoes."

"I need some new shoes. I have a hammertoe. Think they would work for me?" Bertha asked.

"I don't know. But they sure feel good on my bunions." Weenie offered.

"Okay, Bertha, I don't even know what a hammertoe is, but I'm guessing you couldn't make a run for it if needed?"

Bertha cocked her head as if debating the proper answer.

"Bertha can move pretty quick when she's rounding up her cows," Sylvia added.

"Dove, we have to get a move on." Agnes sighed heavily. "Why don't we do this? We can drop you off at Gertrude's house with Donna…"

"Why me?" Donna cringed.

"Because you and Weenie are in the best shape of us all. Weenie, do you feel up to this? I don't want your bunions to give you fits tomorrow." Agnes gave her friend a look of concern.

"I'm ready. I'll be sure to soak my feet when we get back." Weenie grinned from ear to ear.

"Elizabeth, Lorraine and Sylvia will stay here at the house. You guys will keep in contact with us by cell phone. Mildred, you will stay here, too." Agnes stated.

Mom shook her head. "I'm coming, too. I'm not staying here."

"No. If something happens and we both get caught, then who will run the quilt shop?" I gave my mother a look.

"She's right, Mildred. You need to be as far away from this situation as possible." Donna nodded. "We can take my van. It will fit the rest of us."

"So . . . Agnes, Weenie, Donna, Bertha, Maggie and I will go to the house. I think it would be better if I went in by myself. You could drop me off and park somewhere away from the house. If you see someone coming, give two short honks. I'll come back out."

"We could park toward Wendy Rutherford's house." Donna nodded. "She just inherited the house a few miles from Gertrude's. She's rarely there."

"Good idea."

Petunia let out a bleat.

I looked at the goat. "You stay here."

"I think you should take Petunia. She loves car rides, and I'm trying to expose her to new adventures." Elizabeth said with a smile on her face.

"Bring a goat to a breaking and entering?" I asked.

"Sure. She might come in handy." Agnes grinned. "I picked this up for you. I borrowed it from my niece." Agnes shoved a lock-picking kit into my hands. "Gabriella had ordered this online a few months ago when she kept locking herself out of the house. Figured you'd need it tonight."

I nodded. "We need to get going if we are going to do this."

The ladies who were going with me stood and headed out the front door with the goat in tow.

"It's hard to believe that this is my life right now," I muttered. I grabbed a flashlight out of the junk drawer, shoved Mom's gardening gloves into the back of my jeans pocket, and got in line behind the goat.

CHAPTER 10

"Remember, honk twice if you see someone coming to the house." I glanced at the women before I climbed out of the van.

"Take Bertha and Weenie," Donna stated from behind the steering wheel.

"I don't think…"

"Take them." Donna gave me a stern look. I froze for a second, feeling every inch that high school student daring to disobey a teacher.

"Fine." I relented.

Weenie had already climbed out of the van. She had a headband with a light strapped to it. Her white hair was going in all directions.

I frowned at her.

"You like my headlamp? I got it from Amazon. It's perfect for when I read at night in bed." She grinned from ear to ear.

"Weenie, is that camo paint under your eyes?"

"No. I didn't have any. So I found an old tin of shoe polish and used it." She blinked.

"I see." My confidence in my attempt to actually find any clues tonight was slowly waning. I had more of a chance of ending up in the ER with one of the ladies having a heart attack.

"Let's get a move on. Don't have all night, you know." Bertha grumped and dusted off the front of her muumuu, where she'd gathered crumbs from eating cookies in the car.

Weenie and Bertha were like night and day. Weenie was petite and thin as a rail. She usually wore nice but comfortable shoes. Her shoulder-length blonde hair was now completely gray and was always uncontrollable. She had a quirky side to her I liked.

Bertha was twice the size of Weenie and a foot taller. She wore muumuus whenever she could except to church, where she'd wear the same dull brown pantsuit and flats with knee-high stockings that always seemed to roll themselves down to her ankle. She complained about everything and had zero cooking skills. Everyone steered clear of Bertha's casserole whenever there was a potluck at church. She'd been married five times. It was rumored all her husbands died of food poisoning. Whether that was true or not, I wasn't going to find out.

"Let's synchronize our time." Agnes held up her cell phone from the passenger's seat. "You have thirty minutes. Less, if we see someone."

I nodded and checked the time on my cell phone.

Maggie stuck her head out the window from the back seat. "Hey, be sure to check out her underwear drawer."

"Underwear drawer?" I frowned.

"Yes. I was watching a crime show last night, you know, to prepare, and the victim kept all her secrets written in a journal in her underwear drawer." Maggie nodded.

I shook my head and sighed. What in the world had I gotten myself into?

"Keep your phone on vibrate." Donna looked at me.

"I will. Wish us luck," I said.

Petunia poked her head out of the window and bleated.

I watched as the van slowly pulled away and headed down the dark, lonely road.

I looked at Weenie and then Bertha. "Let's go."

By the time we made it up the driveway, Bertha had complained of her toe hurting, and Weenie couldn't stop chatting because of the sugar and the excitement. I was ready to get this over with and go home before someone caught us doing something illegal.

"Hold your headlamp on the doorknob, Weenie, while I try to pick the lock."

"Is it even locked?" Bertha grumped. "Bet those cops forgot to lock it when they left."

I frowned and shoved my hands in the garden gloves. I tried the doorknob. It turned.

"I wasn't expecting it to be that easy."

"Maybe the killer is already inside? What if he's

waiting to kill us because we are on to him? Or her? Women can be murderers, too." Weenie said in a small voice.

My heart pounded in my chest, and my hands began to shake.

"Oh my gosh, you two are such chickens." Bertha shoved past us and walked into the house.

"Bertha!" I hissed, but she had disappeared into the dark house.

"Well, it's now or never." Weenie headed inside, her light bopping along the walls.

"They're going to give me a heart attack," I muttered but followed Weenie inside and slowly closed the door.

I shone my flashlight around the first room I was in. It was the living room. It shocked me to see the amount of antique furniture crammed into the room. It didn't look like someone's house. It looked like a room for storing furniture to be sold.

Weenie appeared at my side.

"I had no idea Gertrude had so many antiques."

"She didn't inherit them." Weenie glared. "That old bat probably stole them." Weenie let out a gasp.

"What?" I glanced around, my senses on high alert.

"There." She pointed to a table in the corner. She walked over, almost tripping on a box of papers. Weenie picked up a mahogany box.

"It's my mother's jewelry box. I knew Louie stole it when he broke into my house." She opened the lid. The tinkle of music filled the dark space.

"Turn that off," I whispered loudly.

Weenie shut the box and the house filled with eerie silence.

"I don't even know where to start looking." I shook my head. Suddenly, there was a crash.

Weenie jerked her head to me and tightened her hold on the box. "What was that?" Her light caught me in the eyes, temporarily blinding me. I squinted and backed away. Something caught my foot, and I fell.

"What are y'all doing? You're making more noise than a preacher at a revival meeting." Bertha towered over me with a grimace.

"We heard a noise" I got to my feet and caught my breath.

"That was me. I was investigating her refrigerator and the butter dish fell out."

"Why in the world are you looking in her refrigerator?" I noticed the pockets on her muumuu were full of something.

"I need some items. Haven't had time to go grocery shopping."

Weenie gasped. "Bertha, you can't take things from someone's refrigerator. The Bible says thou shall not steal."

"The Bible also says to practice hospitality. Besides, she's dead. It would just go to waste." Bertha huffed and made her way back to the kitchen.

"That woman," Weenie shook her head. "Where should we look, Dove?"

"Let's try her bedroom." I led the way down the long hallway, peeking into rooms that held more antique furniture. The rooms looked like it had been a long time since they'd been used as proper bedrooms.

"Maybe this is it." I opened the last door to the right. Inside the small room was a full-size bed, bedside table, and a chest of drawers. This room, unlike the others, was uncluttered.

I stepped inside with Weenie right behind me. I went to the bedside table and opened a drawer, using my flashlight to help me see. The drawer was full of letters and an old book. I picked it up and shone my flashlight on it.

It was A Tale of Two Cities by Charles Dickens. I certainly hadn't thought Gertrude was into classics. I flipped open a few pages. Three photos fell out of the book and onto the floor. I bent and picked them up.

It was a photograph of Eleanor coming out of the back of a building late at night.

"Look at this." I held it out to Weenie to examine.

"That's Sylvia and Maggie's salon." Weenie frowned. "Eleanor owns the building next door to their salon. She's been trying to buy it from Sylvia and Maggie for years. But they refuse to sell to her."

"So she has no business being on their property late at night. I wonder if Gertrude wasn't trying to blackmail Eleanor with these photos."

Weenie's eyebrows shot up. "If it got out that Eleanor had illegally entered someone's property, she would be ostracized."

"And probably face criminal charges." I added. "That would be a motive to kill."

Just then Weenie's phone started singing Nat King Cole's The Christmas Song.

"Weenie, turn that off!"

She shoved the box into my arms and dug around in her Fannie pack.

"Is that your ringtone?"

"Yes."

"Why did you put a Christmas song as your ringtone?" I asked.

She pulled out the phone, and turned the volume off. "Cause Christmas is my favorite holiday." She frowned as she studied the screen. "It's Maggie."

"Good grief, answer it." I hissed and went to look out the window.

"Hello? Is everything alright out there?"

I spotted a light bobbing, coming closer to the house.

"Oh, dear."

"Oh, dear what?" I looked over my shoulder at Weenie. "Is that light one of the ladies coming over here?"

"No. It's not them. We need to leave now." Weenie squealed and opened the bedroom window. Like a flash she was out the window.

I hurried to the kitchen. "Bertha, we have to leave." The back door was opened. Bertha was gone. I realized I was in the house alone.

I heard the sound of breaking glass from the living room. I switched off my flashlight and hurried to the bedroom. I held my breath as footsteps echoed behind me in the house. I realized I couldn't climb out the window holding Weenie's music box. I threw the music box on the bed, scrambled out the window, and ran to the cover of the trees. I squatted behind a large tree and looked back at the house.

"What am I doing? I'm dressed in black. They can't see me." I stood, stepping out away from the tree to get a better look at who was there.

Suddenly I saw a light in the bedroom I had fled. A dark figure with long hair stuck their head out and shone a flashlight across the backyard.

Frightened, I stepped back behind the tree, waiting for what seemed like an eternity.

A limb broke and I swung around. A bright light was beamed in my eyes. I threw up my hands and prayed for courage to face the killer.

"You okay, Dove?" Weenie asked.

I squinted and looked at her. She moved the light out of my eyes. "Weenie? Holy crap. I thought you were the killer. You scared me to death.

"Sorry about that. When Maggie told us to skedaddle, I did just that. I'm older and have bunions so I needed a head start."

"Where's Bertha?"

"She's back at the van. She beat me there. You know, Dove, I don't think Bertha is being honest about having a hammertoe. No way could she have beaten me to the van first."

I shook my head. "Thank God you found me. Since

I'm dressed in black, it's a miracle you spotted me in the first place."

"You were easy to find, Dove." Weenie laughed, pointing to my shirt.

I glanced down. In the dark, the white bone on my shirt glowed. "You've got to be kidding me. Why didn't you tell me I was wearing a glow-in-the-dark shirt?"

Weenie shrugged. "I thought. You knew. I figured you wore it so you could be found quickly."

My stomach sunk as I glanced at the house. It was completely dark inside.

"Whoever that was is gone. But Agnes said they didn't honk because they didn't see the person until it was too late. Maggie swears it was Gertrude's neighbor Wendy. But I don't think so because she is supposed to be out of town."

"Let's get back to the van. We need to get home."

On the ride home, we all sat in silence. The others seemed tired either from the excitement or all that sugar they had consumed. I, on the other hand, was on edge.

I had almost been discovered, and if Agnes was right, we just added another suspect to the list.

CHAPTER 11

It was my turn to make a grocery run, not to mention I was out of my favorite chocolate chip cookies. So I sucked down my coffee and headed over to Mac's grocery store to pick up a few things.

Once I parked, killed the engine and waited for the backfire and plume of smoke to clear from my tailpipe. Only two people were in the parking lot and both of them jumped at the noise. After I stifled my embarrassment and grabbed a shopping cart and headed into the air-conditioned store. The cool air on my hot skin made me grateful I didn't have to work outside in the hot Mississippi heat.

I pushed my cart with its wonky wheel, onto the produce aisle and stopped at the tomatoes. I picked one up, squeezed it, and cringed. "Definitely not." I made a mental note to run over to Agnes' house later to see if she had some fresh tomatoes.

A flash of black caught my attention out of the

corner of my eye. My head snapped in that direction and I froze.

Eleanor Simmons.

She was carefully examining a cantaloupe in her skinny hands.

My heart thumped loudly in my chest, and I bit my lip. I could duck down the next aisle and avoid seeing her or I could be brave, and walk over and talk to her. I might discover something that would help solve the case.

I swallowed my fear and forced my legs to move in that direction.

The sound of my wobbly wheel had her slowly turning in my direction. She almost sneered when she saw me.

I fixed a smile on my face. "Good morning, Eleanor."

"Is it?" She arched a sharp eyebrow. I briefly wondered if anyone had ever thought she had a passing resemblance to Maleficent from the fairy tale.

"I'm just here picking up some groceries for my mom."

"Why would you think I would care?" She stared at me with stony eyes.

Okay, so I pretty much sounded like an idiot. I cleared my throat and approached this from a different angle.

"I was wondering if you could give me some advice."

"That is highly doubtful." She looked back at her cantaloupe.

"Yes, well… I'm thinking about buying a property and fixing it up. I think I want to rent it out. But I've heard that renters can be a nightmare."

Silence.

"Plus, I don't know how much money I could make from it."

She set the cantaloupe down, turning her full attention to me. "It's people like you that think they can be business owners. You obviously have no experience, so what would make you think it's something you could do?"

I snorted. "Gertrude owned some rental properties, so it can't be that hard."

Eleanor sniffed. "Gertrude was a fool. She has a couple of rental houses and that God-awful trailer park that she tried to pass off as an RV oasis. She had more than one unhappy customer. She had a terrible run-in with one of her customers the day she died. The woman demanded Gertrude give her the money back she'd paid for a month's stay. Gertrude refused as usual. She should have sold it to me and I would have made it into something special. Alas, she is dead, and my money is still in my pocket." She examined an extremely long, sharp fingernail.

"You offered to buy her RV park?" I frowned. This was news to me and I suspect the Harland Creek quilters.

"Yes. Now that she's gone, I'll pick it up once they

read the will. I'm sure Winston will sell everything off at a discount. Seems like I came out better in the end."

I opened my mouth to say that Louie was the beneficiary of the will, but thought better of it. No one really knew until the will was actually read.

"Is there anything else?" She narrowed her eyes at me.

"Yes. What do you know about Sylvia and Maggie's building? They are getting older, so the upkeep on a building that age will get expensive."

Anger flashed behind Eleanor's eyes, and she leaned close to me. "Did they say something to you about wanting to sell?"

I stepped back and held out my hands. "No, nothing like that. I was just thinking."

She relaxed a little. "You would do better to keep your mind on not going to jail for murder." She smirked. "Now, if you will excuse me, I have to be going. And Dove? Just because this is a small town doesn't mean bad things can't happen to those who stick their noses where it doesn't belong." She set her cantaloupe in her basket and turned down the aisle.

I waited until she disappeared before pulling out my phone.

Eleanor had mentioned a disgruntled customer at the RV park. I pulled up Dean's phone number and told him to meet me in the parking lot of Mac's ASAP.

Afterward, I stuck my phone back in my jeans pocket and quickly finished my shopping. By the time I was pushing my cart toward my car, I spotted Dean, leaning up against the side of his police car. The snout of a large dog peered out the backseat window.

"That was quick." I popped the trunk of my car and started packing my groceries. "Who's the dog? Does he belong to you?"

"That's Tarzan. He's the new K9 dog for Harland Creek. Just got out of training." He took the bags out of my hand and loaded my trunk. The simple gesture wasn't lost on me. It made my heart tug a little in my chest.

"He looks mean." I cocked my head and took a step toward the dog.

The dog immediately let out a string of aggressive barks. I jumped back.

"He's not a pet, Dove."

"Noted." I eased back to my car.

"So what's the emergency?" He loaded the last bag and shut the trunk.

"I wondered if you had talked to Eleanor about Gertrude's death?"

"I have. While I don't think she had a motive to kill Gertrude, I will keep her on my list."

"I just spoke to Eleanor. She divulged that she offered to buy Gertrude's RV park, but Gertrude to refused to sell. Now that she's dead, Eleanor seems to think she will now get the RV park at a great price since Winston will be selling off everything for drugs. Maybe that's why she killed her." I frowned. "And by the way, have you found the murder weapon yet?"

"You'll be happy to know that nothing in the quilt shop is the murder weapon."

"That's because I didn't kill her."

He cocked his head. "Maybe you moved the murder weapon."

I rolled my eyes.

A black Mercedes drove by slowly. The window went down and Eleanor glared as she passed me.

I spun around and looked at Dean. "What about that? Did you see how she looked at me?"

"Dove, please. Stay out of the investigation. Let us do our jobs, okay?"

He got into his car and drove away.

CHAPTER 12

I had started quilting a Nine Patch quilt when Patricia poked her head in. "Sorry to bother you, Dove. But your mom ran to the bank, and we have a few customers."

I smiled. "Need some help?"

Relief spread across her face. "Yes, please."

"I'll be happy to help." I followed her out to the front of the shop. The soft sound of music drifted through the store. My mom always liked to play music as customers shopped. She said it made them happy, and happy people buy more fabric.

I still hadn't asked Mom about how her business was faring. We were almost done with the quilt orders, and we had no new orders come in since I had been there. Harland Creek was a small town, and so demand would be low. I had played around with the idea of setting up a Facebook business page. People from all states could send in their pieced quilts to be quilted and once finished, we would ship them back. I figured it would be a good idea.

Patricia was busy cutting up some floral fabric by Moda for Elizabeth, while Maggie and Lorraine discussed which backing they should get for a Churn Dash quilt Lorraine had finished piecing.

I spotted an unfamiliar woman with short platinum blonde hair, and green eyes standing at the counter, tapping her ballet flat while glaring at Patricia.

I walked up to her and smiled. "Hi, can I help you?"

As she pursed her lips together for a second, she narrowed her eyes. My guard immediately went up.

"Do you have the Tula Pink Fabric?"

Ah, Tula Pink. The fabric line is known for its bright and busy colors.

"We usually keep that fabric along the wall over there. I'll show you." I walked past the batiks and stopped when I spotted the bright fabric with flamingos. "Here we are. Is there a specific color or pattern you are looking for?"

She glanced down at the fabric and then shook her head. "I need the one with the butterflies on the green background. I think it's called Tiny Beasts."

"We sold the last yard yesterday. But we have some ordered."

She crossed her arms and glared. "How long will that take?"

I frowned. "We usually get our fabrics within a

week of ordering." I cocked my head. "I'm sorry, but you don't look familiar. Are you passing through?"

"I wish," she gritted through her teeth.

"If you want to leave your name and number, I can call when it comes in."

She let out a heavy sigh. "Fine."

I headed to the counter to get a pen and piece of paper. "What's your name?"

"Polly O'Hara."

I scribbled her name down on the paper and looked up. "And do you have a good number to reach you?"

"The cell service where I'm staying is awful." She gave me her number anyway.

"I can contact you by email or message you on Facebook if you have access to a computer."

She pursed her lips. "That stupid RV park doesn't have Wi-Fi either."

I looked at Polly. "You aren't staying at the Chateau RV Park, are you?"

'The one and the same. And I've been trying to call that awful owner to get my money back. But it seems like I'm stuck until my royalty check comes in."

I frowned. "Your royalty check?"

She lifted her chin in the air. "Yes. I'm a writer."

Lorraine eased over to where we were standing. "I'm sorry to barge in, but did I overhear you say your name is Polly O'Hara?"

"Yes, it is."

Lorraine's eyes grew wide. "Are you the author?"

A slight smile tugged on Polly's mouth. "Yes, I am."

Lorraine grinned from ear to ear. "I have read all your romance books."

Polly preened under the praise. "That's good to hear."

"I had no idea you were in Harland Creek. Are you here doing research?" Lorraine's face lit with excitement.

Polly snorted. "If staying at a rundown RV park is research, then yes."

Lorraine gasped. "You're not staying there, are you?"

"Unfortunately, yes. I've been trying to get in contact with that owner to refund my money so I can find a different area to stay, but it goes straight to voicemail."

Lorraine pressed her lips together and looked at me. I knew from the look Lorraine was giving me, she expected me to tell Polly the unpleasant truth why she couldn't get in touch with Gertrude.

I cleared my throat. "Mrs. O'Hara…"

"It's Ms. I'm recently divorced. That son of a… I mean, my ex-husband, John, got half of my money and half of the royalties from books I wrote while married."

"That's awful. I mean, he certainly didn't write them, did he?" Lorraine frowned.

Polly looked offended. "Absolutely not. That idiot couldn't even write a picture book. He didn't even read any of the books I wrote. I got the camper while he got the house. It wasn't fair, but he and the judge were high school buddies." She sneered. "I'm here for a month, trying to write this next book. On top of that, I'm behind schedule and I have another book due in two months. I spent the last of my savings on my spot at the RV park."

"Wow, you must be a very prolific writer," I said.

She shifted her weight and averted her eyes.

"With all that writing, when do you find time to quilt?" I asked.

"At night, when I'm thinking of how I'll write the next scene. Right now, I'm working on a new cozy quilting mystery. I don't think it's going to sell well. But it's what my publisher wants."

"I see."

"Dove, tell her." Lorraine gave me a look.

"Tell me what?" Polly narrowed her eyes.

"You're not going to get in touch with the owner."

"And why is that?" Polly glared.

"Because she's dead."

Polly's eyes widened. She went white. "Dead? But I didn't shove her that har…" She slammed her mouth shut, looking from me to Lorraine.

The room suddenly became quiet.

"You what?" I leaned forward. Did Polly just accidentally admit to shoving Gertrude? What would make Polly that upset to get physical with the old woman?

"Nothing. I have to go." Polly ran out of the shop.

I raced to the window with Lorraine on my heels. We pressed our faces to the glass and stared in horror as Polly O'Hara, the romance author, squealed tires out of the parking lot.

When she was gone, Lorraine looked at me and blinked.

"Another suspect?" She asked.

"Looks like the suspects are growing every day." I shook my head and looked out the window.

CHAPTER 13

I finished the Nine Patch Quilt an hour after closing, then called Dean to tell him what Polly O'Hara had said, but my call went straight to voicemail. Irritated that he wasn't taking me seriously, I didn't bother leaving a message.

I drove home in silence. I had too much on my mind to even listen to music.

A murder had occurred in my mom's shop.

I was the number one suspect.

Dean wasn't taking me seriously about the clues I was finding.

Mom's quilt shop was struggling, and she hadn't told me.

Not to mention the fact my career was over and I was back home living with my mom. I wasn't even sure what I was supposed to do next with my life.

Would I become like Patricia, over fifty years old and living at home with her mother?

All I wanted was to soak in a hot bubble bath and let the weight of the world fall from my shoulders, even if just for a minute.

When I got home, Mom had already left to meet up with her quilting friends. They were all headed over to Elizabeth Harland's house to have dinner. I was invited, but I politely declined.

I needed some time to myself.

After a long soak in my lavender bubble bath, I threw on some denim cut-off shorts and a white T-shirt I'd miraculously found in the back of my closet.

I grabbed my Mac laptop and went downstairs to make myself something to eat.

I scanned the refrigerator and found some leftover chicken salad Mom had made. I quickly toasted some Rye bread and to make myself a sandwich. Taking my plate with my glass of sweet tea into the living room, I settled onto the couch.

Opening my computer, I did a quick search of all the fabric shops that offered quilting in Mississippi. I checked to see if they had a Facebook page. There were only four that had a Facebook page.

A smile formed on my face as an idea sprouted, one that could really make a difference and perhaps turn things around for my mom and her quilting shop.

I could set up a Facebook page and show Mom how to use it. She also needed an updated website, but that was out of my wheelhouse. I remembered Agnes telling me her niece was good at marketing. I grabbed a piece of paper out of my purse to make a note to contact her about whether she could help set up a new and user-friendly website.

As I ate, I worked on setting up a social media page for Mildred's Quilt Shop. Photos of quilts we had quilted at the shop were perfect for the banner. I picked a double wedding ring quilt, a morning star quilt and an Irish chain quilt. They had all been detailed quilted, not to mention the colors were gorgeous and very eye-catching.

At least now we could reach a wider audience, and potential customers could message us for a quote on quilting based on the size.

I hadn't been on Facebook in a while and noticed I had a lot of messages. I quickly went through them. They were all from people, former friends, I knew in New York. Most of them were not nice, so I decided not to answer.

Was Dean on Facebook? He didn't seem the type to be active on social media.

I started to shut down my computer, but my curiosity got the better of me. I typed in his name and quickly found him.

His profile was a photo of Tarzan, the dog he said he just got. Maybe he was on social media more than I thought?

I pulled up his friend list. There were a lot of people from high school I recognized, along with many cops that I didn't know.

Next, I scrolled through his photos. There were several photos of him with his family and a couple of him in uniform at a police charity event.

I scrolled to the next photo and froze. There was a pretty brunette sitting on his lap at a picnic table. In the background were a tent and a fire. They were dressed in winter clothes and it appeared they were camping.

Something squeezed my heart. Who was this woman?

I clicked on the photo to see if the woman was tagged.

She wasn't.

I scrolled through the comments under the photo.

Bingo.

The woman's name was Samantha Vaughn, and she'd left a comment.

"Thanks for a night to remember under the stars."

I gaped at the picture. It seems Dean hadn't been pining for me all these years, after all.

I slammed the computer shut and put it on the coffee table.

There was a knock at the door.

I was in no mood for visitors. I headed to the front door and flung it open without looking to see who was on the other side.

My heart nearly stopped when I saw Dean standing there.

"What are you doing here?" I demanded. I felt like he'd caught me with my hand in the cookie jar, so to speak.

He arched an eyebrow. "I saw where you called. You

should have left a message, and I would have gotten back to you sooner."

"Didn't want to bother you. Between work and your social life, I figured you didn't have time to be answering my calls." My eyes dropped to his lips, and I wondered if he had kissed Samantha Vaughn the way he used to kiss me.

"Whatever that means." He didn't bother waiting for an invitation but barged past me. "You by yourself?"

"Yes." I closed the door. "Mom is at Elizabeth's house for dinner."

"Oh, yes. The quilting club's once-a-month dinner. They all take turns hosting."

"All except Bertha." I added.

He frowned. "I always wondered how they managed to hide it from her."

I walked into the living room. "Mom said they usually do it impromptu. Whoever is hosting will send out a group text that day where it will be held."

"That's pretty stealthy, isn't it? And what if someone has plans for that night?"

"They're all widowed. Or divorced. It's not like they have much of a nightlife." I narrowed my eyes. "Unlike you." I eased on the couch, waiting for him to take the bait and offer up some information on his personal life.

Instead of sitting in the recliner, he sat on the couch next to me.

I shifted in my seat.

"Dove, I need to ask you something."

I rolled my eyes. I should have known he wouldn't talk about himself. "No. I did not murder Gertrude."

He snorted. "Not that. I want to know why you are back in Harland Creek."

"Does it matter?"

"Yes." His eyes hardened on me.

"Fine. My life didn't turn out like I thought it would. I had no place else to go. So I came home."

"No boyfriend?"

"Not anymore," I muttered, wondering why it mattered to him.

He stiffened at my words. "Was it serious?"

"I thought it was. But when things got rough, he didn't stick around." I shrugged.

"What did he do for a living?"

"He was an heir to a vineyard in France. So he didn't have to work."

"An heir? That's pretty fancy. You always were drawn to the finer things in life." He smirked.

"Whatever that means." I shook my head. "Doesn't matter anyhow. With this case still unsolved and Mom's business hurting for customers, my personal life is the last thing on my mind." I shifted on the couch to get a better look at him. "Why don't you let me help you investigate the case?"

"Because you will get in the way. A murder investigation is no place for you." He shrugged. "Besides, I'm sure you'll be happier focusing on your social life and activities."

"It's Harland Creek. What kind of social life am I

supposed to have?" I smirked. "What about you? Anyone special?"

"I'm too busy working to be dating." He laughed.

"Oh, I wouldn't be so sure about that. I'm sure you've had plenty of dates since we were a couple. Probably some outdoors type who loved to go hunting with you. You know, someone who fits into your life. Someone fond of being under the stars." I smirked.

He grew serious and stared into my eyes. "Dove, I never expected you to do things you didn't enjoy, like hunting with me."

I stiffened and jabbed my finger at him. "As I recall, you took me duck hunting when it snowed and when our boat started taking on water, you got mad at me for being scared." I pointed at him.

"You were trying to climb out of the boat and swim back to shore. I wasn't mad. I was trying to keep you from killing yourself." He glared as if daring me to challenge his assertion.

"What about the time you wanted to go camping, and I kept hearing a noise outside the tent? You got mad and packed everything up and drove me back home. Don't tell me you weren't mad then?" I cocked my head.

He stood up. "I was mad because I was trying to get some sleep and you kept poking me in the side every time an acorn fell."

I jumped up. "See! You got mad!"

He shoved his hand through his thick hair and growled. "Dove, you are the most infuriating woman I have ever known. No wonder a man won't stick around." He stomped out of the house and slammed the door behind him.

I jumped at the sound.

I fisted my hands at my sides, thoroughly convinced that romance was very overrated.

I shoved away the thought that maybe Dean was right. Maybe I was destined to be alone for the rest of my life.

Shaking my head, I headed into the kitchen to drown my frustrations in some rocky road ice cream.

CHAPTER 14

"Dove, you need to see this," my mom called out from her office.

I could tell from the tone in her voice something wasn't right. I stepped away from the longarm machine and into her office.

I frowned. "What's up?"

She was sitting at her desk looking at her Facebook page on the computer. Agnes was standing behind her looking over her shoulder. "We are getting messages."

I smiled. "Oh, that's good. Are they asking about quilting services?"

"No. They are asking is it true that a murder took place here." Mom grimaced at me. "I'm not sure what to say."

"Oh, my gosh." I cupped my face in my hands, horrified that my marketing skills were backfiring. "I didn't even think people would find out about that."

"Look at that. This woman is claiming to be a

medium. She says she can come into the shop and commune with the dead. She is saying she can find out who the murderer is."

Mom pointed at the screen. "She says she'll only charge eight hundred dollars."

Agnes huffed. "That's a scam. I met a woman in New Orleans that read my palm one time. She only charged twenty bucks. Plus she was wrong about everything. Told me I was going to marry my enemy." Agnes let out a laugh. "I'm never marrying again even if someone paid me a million dollars."

Mom looked up at me with worry in her eyes. "What am I going to do? Should I respond?"

I shook my head. "No. I'll respond. Just ignore the ones wanting to know about the murder for now."

For the rest of the morning, I combed through the messages. I skipped over the ones wanting details about the murder. When I came upon legitimate questions about prices, I quoted amounts for quilting options. By the time I'd finished, I had three confirmed customers. Perhaps a win after all.

My stomach growled and I glanced at the time. It was past noon. I'd missed lunch.

I walked out of the office and spotted Mom and Patricia with their heads together talking about something. When I walked over, they both looked up.

"Is everything okay?"

Mom gave me a nervous look. "Patricia's received a threatening letter."

"Patricia?" I looked at her, clearly worried. "What did it say?"

She swallowed and looked at me with big eyes behind her cat glasses. "You can read it." She held out the letter with the envelope.

I took the papers from her trembling hand and carefully read the letter.

Better leave the quilt shop before something happens to you, too.

I turned over the envelope to investigate where the post office stamp originated. Alarmed by what I saw, I looked at her. "It was mailed from Harland Creek."

"Patricia, if you want to take some vacation time until this is sorted out, I will understand."

"I can't do that, Mildred. I need my paycheck." She turned her worried eyes on my mom.

"Well, maybe I can pay you for your time off." Mom bit her lip.

"Mom, can you afford to do that?" I looked at her.

"A week at the most. After that I'll need you back here in the shop, Patricia."

Patricia let out a grateful sigh. "Oh, thank you so much. I know you'll get this mess sorted out and it will be back to business as usual."

Mom gave her a strained smile. "Can you finish out the day and start your paid week off tomorrow?"

"Of course." Patricia turned back to the cutting mat. "I can get these charm packets cut before the day is out."

Mom gave me a look that meant something was on

her mind. I quietly followed her back to her office. She shut the door behind me.

"Dove, I have to tell you something."

"I think I know what you're going to say. The business isn't doing as well as it should. You're having money issues. Now you're going to be working short-handed with Patricia being out of the shop for a week."

She nodded silently. "I didn't tell you because I didn't want you to worry." Her brows furrowed.

I sighed heavily. "I think we just have to keep plugging on. We did get some quilt orders from our new Facebook page. They should be arriving in a few days."

"That's good." Mom gave me a small smile.

"It is. I think everything will end up turning around." I reassured her.

"Who do you think sent that letter? The killer?"

I shook my head. "I don't know. What I do know is no one is safe until the killer is found. You know, when we went to Gertrude's house, Agnes said that she swore it was Gertrude's neighbor, Wendy, that was in her house. I think I need to go have a chat with her."

"I don't know if she's at home or not. And I'm not sure how I feel about you going by yourself."

"I'll be fine. Wendy may have an idea about Gertrude and her habits. She might know more about her neighbor than anyone. Do you mind if I take off the rest of the day?"

"Not at all. I can start on that Log Cabin quilt that was dropped off yesterday."

I pulled her into a hug. "I should be back in a few hours. If not, send a search party out." I laughed.

Mom grew serious. "Dove, don't say things like that. Not in this tense environment."

"Sorry." I grabbed my purse and keys.

"Oh, I almost forgot. Someone called the house this morning wanting to speak to you. Said they were a friend from New York."

My blood ran cold.

"Did they leave a message?" I squeaked out.

"No. And they didn't leave a name. Said they would call back later." She frowned. "Everything okay? Do you think it's someone wanting to hire you as a buyer in New York? I was surprised when you told me you lost your position at Nordstrom's. I know how much that job meant to you."

I forced a smile to my face. "You're not trying to get rid of me are you?"

"Of course not. I love having you back home. It was always my hope that you'd stay, but I know how you love big city life." She smiled. "I'm going to get started on that Log Cabin."

I hurried out of the door into the stifling heat. My lies were piling up like autumn leaves. I was afraid they would quickly catch fire, leaving behind destruction in their path.

I made it to Wendy Rutherford's house in less than ten minutes. She lived outside the town of Harland Creek down a rural road. I pulled into the driveway of Wendy's small white house with the black shutters. The scent of watermelon hung heavy in the air, letting me know the grass had been recently cut. I was probably the only person in the South that thought cut grass smelled like watermelon. I pulled under the shade of the oak tree and killed the engine.

The garage of the house was down. I couldn't tell if Wendy was home, but I prayed she was. I needed to talk to her.

I killed the engine. It backfired, shooting up a plume of smoke. I was starting to get used to the old car, as it didn't make me jump anymore.

I got out of the car and walked up to the front door. I noticed that Wendy had zero flowers or landscaping around the house. It looked more like a rental house than someone's actual home.

I rapped on the door and waited. When no one answered, I stepped over to the window, cupping my hands together to look inside the darkened house.

The living room was sparsely decorated with a single gray couch along with a wingback chair. There was a lamp on a small table beside the chair. There were no pictures on the wall or decorations that made a house a home.

In fact, there were no signs of life inside at all.

I decided to head to the back of the house to investigate further.

I walked around the side of the house, passing some unkempt pink hydrangea bushes four feet high. The flowers reminded me of my childhood and spending summers at my grandmother's house. Dove Lucille

Smith. My mother named me after my grandmother. As a child I loved it, but when I hit middle school, the kids started making fun of my name, teasing that I was a bird.

.I stopped when I spotted a business card stuck in the screen of the door. I walked over and pulled it out.

Ron Dexter

Dexter Gravel Company

Below it was the number of the business.

I turned it over but there was nothing written on the back.

I pulled out my phone and took a picture of the card. When I got back to town, I would call and talk to Ron to see if I could find out any information.

"Can I help you?"

The unexpected voice caused me to spin around and let out a scream.

"You scared me to death." I pressed my hand to my chest, eyeing the woman in front of me. "You must be Wendy."

"I am. And who are you? And what are you doing on my property?" Her eyes drifted to the card in my hand.

I was trapped. I said the first word that came to my mind without thinking. "I'm Jane. I am here to welcome you to Harland Creek and invite you to church."

That fast-thinking came from the many years my mom would spot a new member who just moved into the neighborhood. She would usually visit within two days with a casserole and an invitation to join us for church service at First Baptist.

She lifted her chin. "I'm not much on church. Was raised an atheist."

"I see." I cleared my throat. "I have to apologize. I usually visit new neighbors and bring a casserole but work has been so hectic, I didn't have time to make something."

She narrowed her eyes. "Where do you work?"

"Mildred's Quilt Shop."

Her eyebrows shot up. "That place where Gertrude was murdered? Have they caught the killer?"

I shook my head. "The police are still investigating. Still no leads on who the suspect is."

She snorted. "I heard it was the owner's daughter."

"That's not true. It's just a rumor." I stated.

She narrowed her eyes on me as if she didn't believe me.

I cleared my throat. "So were you close to Gertrude? I mean you are her nearest neighbor."

Wendy let out a sharp laugh. "Close? Absolutely not. That witch has done everything in her power to make my life miserable."

"Really? I knew she wasn't a very likeable person…"

"Likeable?" Wendy snorted. "I can't think of one person in Harland Creek who had a nice word to say about her."

"That's true," I admitted. "So you didn't see anything suspicious going on at her house?"

"You're very nosey." She cocked her head and narrowed her eyes a bit.

"Well, it's a small town. Not a lot happens here." I shrugged.

"Suspicious activity went on at her house all the time. With that thug, Louie and her no-good nephew Winston, I'm surprised I have anything left in my house that wasn't stolen."

My eyes grew wide. "You had stuff stolen from your house?"

"Yes. A lot of antique furniture that came with the house. I know Gertrude stole it. It was priceless."

How much money was she talking about? Enough money to kill for?

Her eyes narrowed. "What do you have in your hand?"

I glanced down at the business card I was clutching. "Oh, this was stuck in your screen door. I was going to write my name and number on the back but remembered I didn't have a pen."

She held out her hand.

I placed the card in her open palm.

"I should be leaving now." I turned to leave but she grabbed my elbow.

"Not so fast. You didn't tell me your number. You know, in case I change my mind about attending church." She met my eyes.

I blinked. I repeated the number to the quilt shop. She didn't bother writing it down, but I bet my bottom dollar she would be able to remember the number.

"I have to get going. Have a good day." I gave her an awkward smile and trotted back to my car at a fast pace.

When I slid into the driver's seat, I immediately hit the lock button. I started the car and drove straight back to Harland Creek, checking my rearview mirror every few seconds.

CHAPTER 15

"Did any of you go to Gertrude's funeral?" I looked at the quilting ladies who were sitting in the backroom of the quilting shop. It was only eight in the morning and the shop wasn't open until nine. They had all gathered, along with Petunia, to get updates on the investigation.

"No. She had a private funeral. Only Winston, Louie and Gertrude's lawyer attended per her last wishes." Lorraine took a sip of her tea. Agnes had brought some of the fancy tea from The English Rose Bookstore. The owner, Colin, and Agnes's niece were dating and rumors kept floating around that they would soon get married.

"Has the will been read yet?" Mom asked.

"No. Not yet." Donna added. "Her attorney divulged that to me."

"That's because old Stanley has a thing for you." Sylvia teased.

"That's not true." Donna glared.

"Let's get back on track." I cleared my throat. "I have some new information. I went to see Wendy Rutherford."

"Gertrude's neighbor?" Weenie's eyes went wide.

"Yes. She seemed very suspicious to me."

"Did you ask her if she killed Gertrude?" Bertha asked.

"I couldn't very well come out and ask that could I?"

Bertha shrugged. "Perry Mason would ask."

"Weenie, remember we saw all that antique furniture in Gertrude's house?"

"Yes." Weenie nodded.

"Wendy said she knew that Gertrude had stolen all the antique furniture out of the house. From our conversation, I could tell there was a lot of bad blood between them."

"She's definitely a suspect." Maggie narrowed her eyes. "I really think that must be who I spotted going into Gertrude's house the night you broke in. Maybe she was going in to get her furniture."

"She wouldn't give me much information, but I did find a business card in the screen of her backdoor. Dexter Gravel company."

"Hmmm. Interesting." Elizabeth narrowed her eyes. "You know that same company wanted to test for gravel on my land. They told me if they found some they would offer me a good deal of money to have it harvested."

"What did you say?" Sylvia asked.

"I told them to get off my property and never come back. I'm a flower farmer. I can't grow flowers in gravel." She shook her head.

"I'm going to head over there today to see if I can find out any information." I looked at my mom. "I know you are working short-handed since Patricia isn't here for the week."

"Your mother told me about that stupid letter." Agnes scowled. "Did she take it to Dean?"

I nodded. "We told her to."

"I can't believe Patricia is such a coward. She should have thrown that letter in the garbage and simply forgot about it." Agnes scowled.

"Patricia can't help it. She's always been so emotional." Mom sighed and looked at me. "It's fine, honey. You go do what you need to do."

"It's in Jackson, so it will take me an hour to get there and an hour to get back." I frowned, worried I was leaving her in a bind.

"I'll be glad to stay and help." Donna offered with a smile. "I can't longarm quilt, like you Dove. But I can assist customers and cut fabric."

"Yes, and I can hang around, too, and help bind some quilts. Heather has everything covered at the farm, but I will need someone to take care of Petunia." Elizabeth scratched the goat between her ears.

Petunia let out a bleat.

"I'll go with Dove, and we'll take Petunia with us." Agnes smiled.

"Wait, what? You can't take a goat to Jackson."

"Why not? She's been to Natchez." Agnes argued with a frown.

"Yes, take Agnes and Petunia with you. I would feel a lot better if you didn't go alone." Mom worried her lip with her teeth.

"Fine, but she better not poop in my car." I could not believe I had agreed to ride a goat around in my car like some lapdog.

Minutes later we were in my car with me driving with Agnes in the passenger's seat, and Petunia in the back. Agnes insisted on listening to the Oldies station on the radio. Luckily, we only had to stop once so Petunia could do her business and Agnes could get something to eat at a gas station.

By the time we pulled into the parking lot of Dexter's Gravel, Agnes was groaning.

"My stomach is killing me." Agnes moaned.

"It's probably that gas station hot dog. It looked a little off to me. If you feel bad, is Petunia going to be sick, too? You bought her a hot dog too." The truth was the hot dog looked green. I tried to warn Agnes but she said she was craving a hot dog and wasn't going to let my warning stop her.

"Petunia has a cast iron stomach. Nothing bothers her. I can't say the same about me. I've got to get to a bathroom, quick." She was out the door, heading into the Dexter Gravel office before I could get my seatbelt off.

"Great. Now who's going to watch you?" I looked at Petunia.

Petunia gave a bleat.

"I can't leave you in the car. It's too hot." I rubbed my temples. "Maybe I can pass you off as a comfort animal." I looked at the goat. "Can you behave yourself?"

Petunia blinked.

"We don't have all day. Let's go." I got out of the car and opened the backdoor. Petunia hopped out and I grabbed her leash before she could gnaw on it.

I walked up to the entrance of Dexter Gravel and opened the front door. I stepped inside and the welcome breeze of the air conditioner greeted me.

"Can I help you? I'm afraid if you're looking for a bathroom it's already occupied." The young blond receptionist cast a worried look off to the right. I assumed that's where the bathroom was and I was pretty sure Agnes was wreaking havoc in it.

"No, I don't need a bathroom."

The secretary glanced down at Petunia, spotting the goat for the first time. "I'm sorry but animals aren't allowed inside."

"She's not just an animal. She's a service animal."

The receptionist frowned. "I thought service animals wore vests."

"She got something on hers and it's at the dry cleaners." I held my breath to see if she would buy it.

"Oh." She blinked and then looked back at me, seeming reluctant to argue with anything I just said. "Do you have an appointment?"

"I'm here to see Ron Dexter. It concerns some land

in Harland Creek." I hoped that would bait him into agreeing to meet with me.

She picked up the phone and punched in some numbers. When she hung up, she gave me a smile.

"He said he'll see you right away. Just go down the hall and it's the first door to the right."

"Thank you." I smiled. My bluff worked.

I headed down the hallway with Petunia in tow. When we got to Ron's office, I peeked inside.

"You're not who I expected to see." Ron Dexter, who wore a gray suit and had his black hair slicked back, stood from behind his desk and walked around.

"Sorry about that. My name is Dove Agnew. And I have some questions about your interest in a certain land in Harland Creek."

"You're talking about Wendy Rutherford's land. Are you friends with her?"

"We are acquaintances."

"I'm sorry, Miss Agnew. I can't discuss confidential contracts or offers made. I'm sorry." He gave me a stern look, and I knew there was no way I was getting any info out of him.

His gaze drifted down to my side and cringed. "Is that a goat?"

Petunia took one look at him and started hacking.

"Oh, no. I think she's going to be sick. Is there a bathroom?"

"She can't be sick in here! This is a place of business."

I picked up a garbage can and held it up to her mouth. "Where's the closest bathroom!"

"Down the hall to the left!" He pulled out a handkerchief and held it to his nose.

I picked up Petunia and ran down the hall to the bathroom. I made it just in time. I held the goat's head over the toilet while she yacked up the gas station hot dog.

When she was done, I set her down. She blinked and looked up at me.

"I thought you had a cast iron stomach."

She bleated.

I wiped her mouth with a paper towel and then proceeded to wash my hands. As I was drying them, Petunia nudged the door open, escaping out of the bathroom.

"Petunia!" I gritted out and ran after the stubborn goat.

I saw her tail dart into a room next to the bathroom. I made sure no one was in the hallway before following her.

"You are going to get me in trouble." I whispered loudly, stepping into the room with a large desk, piled with papers. "We need to get out of here before they call the cops. Where are you?"

I bent down and spotted Petunia under the table with paper in her mouth.

"Oh my gosh. Will you stop that?" I crawled over to her and pulled the document out of her mouth.

I frowned when I read it. It stated they made an offer to Wendy to lease her land to harvest the gravel off of it. They had tested Gertrude's land as well for gravel, but there wasn't as much as Wendy's. But because their lands joined, Dexter Gravel wanted to lease both properties so they could put a washer in for the gravel.

I couldn't believe what I was reading.

Gertrude would never sell her land. Wendy had motivation to kill Gertrude to buy the land from Louie or Winston. I highly doubted either one would want to keep the property and stay in Harland Creek.

"Petunia, you are a genius."

Petunia let out a burp.

"Let's get out of here." I stuck the papers in my jeans pocket, picked up the goat and carried my new best friend back to the car.

CHAPTER 16

I had dropped Agnes and Petunia off before heading back to the quilt shop. I showed her the paperwork and filled her in on what I had found.

"I had no idea that Dexter Gravel made an offer to Wendy. Gertrude would never lease her land. She doesn't like anyone on her property. Besides, she would get her money in other ways."

"Certainly makes Wendy a suspect."

"Sure does. Let's add her to the list." I headed over to the whiteboard. "What quilt block should we call her?"

Mom pressed her lips together in a thin line and thought for a second. "What about pinwheel? Since we don't really know anything about her?"

"Good one." I smiled as I added her to our list.

"Patricia called. She said she felt bad about not being here this week. I tried to reassure her, but she said she doesn't feel right about getting paid and not working."

"Is she coming back to the shop?" I asked hopefully.

"No. It was obvious how nervous she was over the phone. But I think we can give her something to do at home."

"What do you mean?"

"I was going to deliver some fabric so she can cut them for our prepackaged precuts that people have ordered."

"Does she have everything she needs at home, like a rotary cutter and mat?"

"Yes. All I have to do is drop off the fabric." Mom smiled.

"I'll do it. Just gather the supplies and I'll run it over. That way you can keep working on finishing that binding for the quilt you've been working on. One more finished quilt means money."

Mom sighed heavily. "Yes it does. And thanks, honey. I appreciate it." She went about the task of gathering the bolts of fabric along with the instruction sheet on how much and what size that needed to be cut. Once she finished gathering everything, she put it all in a large tote.

I picked up the tote. "I'll run these over and head back. Is there anything else you need while I'm out?"

"No, I'm good." Mom smiled as she finished ringing up a customer.

I put the tote in my trunk and headed over to Patricia's house.

I pulled up to a small white house a few streets over from where Mom lived. The house looked in dire need of fresh paint and the screen door was hanging at an angle. I set the tote down by the front door and knocked.

It took a few seconds, but Patricia finally opened the door. She seemed surprised to see me.

"Dove." She glanced down at the tote. "I'm sorry it took me so long to get to the door. Mother just finished her bath, and I was helping her get dressed. Come in." She held the door open, and I picked up the tote to carry it inside.

The house was small, but cozy and there were pictures of Patricia as a child.

"Where would you like me to put this?" I looked around.

"Bring it to my room. I have a table set up there." She led the way down the small hallway.

She opened the door, and I was surprised to see how different it looked from the rest of the house. Her room, unlike the other rooms, was updated. There was fresh red paint on the walls and colorful artwork hung. I stopped to admire an acrylic picture of a fiery sunset over what looked like an Indian mosque. Her canopy bed was dark and decorated in an assortment of reds, oranges and yellows in a mandala design. A mosaic lamp sat on her desk beside her computer. Beside her computer was an eight-foot desk with a large cutting mat and rotary cutter.

Patricia pointed. "Just put it on the table."

I set the tote down carefully on the table and turned around to study the room. "I like your room. It's very colorful."

She brightened. "Thank you. I decorated it to make it more like my space. I needed just one room to make my own. As you can tell the rest of the house is Mother's taste. I've tried to get her to let me paint the walls, but she preferred that old outdated wallpaper."

Her computer dinged and Patricia glanced over. "I have another message on Facebook. Don't you just get all excited when you get a message from a friend?" Her face brightened with excitement.

I shrugged."I haven't had time to get on Facebook much since I moved back home."

"I don't think I could live without it. I still keep up with all my friends from high school."She grinned. "I bet a girl as pretty as you had a ton of friends. And boyfriends."

"Dean is the only friend from high school I keep up with."

Patricia's eyes twinkled with mischief. "I heard you two were sweethearts in school."

"We dated but broke up after graduation."

Her face fell. "That must have been hard on you. Him dumping you."

I straightened my shoulders. "Actually, I was the one who broke up with him."

She blinked in disbelief. "Really? Why? He's so handsome and smart and looks really good in that uniform. If I had a man like Dean, I wouldn't let him go."

I shifted my weight, clearly uncomfortable with the direction of this conversation.

Maybe I didn't deserve someone like Dean. Maybe I deserved all the bad stuff happening to me.

"I'm sorry, Dove. I didn't mean to pry. It's just after living with Mother for years, I long for romance. Even if it's from someone else's experience. It's hard to find romance in Harland Creek. Even if I had someone here, there's no romantic places he could take me."

A small smile tugged at the corner of my lips. "Actually there are a lot of romantic places. That lake behind Colin Bennett's house is great for picnics. And I heard Grayson put in a zipline between his land and Elizabeth that goes over Harland Creek."

"Those sound great but not really secluded." Patricia sighed heavily.

"And then there's the old Randal Cabin."

"But no one has lived there for years."

"I know. It used to be a hunting cabin for some man out of Jackson. But during the summers it was the perfect place to get away with your sweetheart." Memories of Dean kissing me on the porch tugged at my heart. It was almost like it was yesterday.

"Sounds like you two had a great time." Patricia giggled.

I cleared my throat and shook my head. "My point is, that it's still not too late for you to get married.

You're special someone is out there just waiting on you."

She brightened at my words. "You really think so?"

"Sure. A lot of the women I met in New York didn't get married until later in life.'

A grin split her face. "Thanks, Dove. I appreciate you saying that. It gives me hope."

"We all need hope."

"Especially you." Patricia grew grim. "I sure am sorry about all the trouble you and your mom are going through. I hope this will soon end and things will get back to normal."

"Me, too." When my cell phone rang, I reached into my pocket and answered it.

"Hello?"

"Dove, as soon as you drop that stuff off at Patricia's, get back to the shop. Dean came by and gave us some new information regarding the investigation."

"Really?" I took a few steps away from Patricia to have a bit more privacy. Patricia was busy unpacking the bolts of fabric and lining them up.

"Dean, said that he went back to talk to Polly O'Hara, that author staying at the RV park, and she finally broke down and admitted to hitting Gertrude."

"She did?"

"Yes. Get back to the shop and I'll fill you in on the rest."

"Everything okay? Nothing else bad has happened, has it?" Patricia gave me a look of concern. When her hand went to her throat, she began worrying the pendant underneath her shirt.

"Everything is fine. Don't worry. I've got to get back to the shop. Thanks for working from home, Patricia. We really appreciate it."

"Anything I can do for Mildred. She's been a godsend. In more ways than one." Patricia gave me a wistful look.

As I drove back to the shop, I was intrigued by this new information regarding Polly O'Hara.

I had a feeling this case was very close to being solved.

CHAPTER 17

"So, are you going to make an arrest?" I looked at Dean. I had driven straight over from Patricia's and found Dean in the backroom of the quilt shop drinking coffee.

He leaned against the counter, took a sip and studied me for a second. "We need evidence or a confession to make an arrest."

"But Polly O'Hara admitted to hitting Gertrude." I propped my hands on my hips.

"She slapped Gertrude. Not hit. And she slapped her at the RV park. She also said the first time she stepped foot into the quilt shop was a few days after the murder."

I crossed my arms over my chest. "She could be lying. She could have followed Gertrude to the shop."

He pushed off the counter and set his coffee cup down. "So how did Gertrude get in the quilt shop if you didn't let her in?"

"I don't know. Maybe she picked the lock? Seems like everyone in Harland Creek has a lock picking kit." I huffed.

He arched his brow. "Do you?"

"No." I narrowed my eyes. It was the truth. I'd given the only one I had in my possession back to Agnes after almost getting caught breaking into Gertrude's house.

"So what would Gertrude want to break into the quilt shop in the first place?"

"She was coming to get her quilt. That crazy woman wanted it done that night. After I finished it, I waited a little bit for her to come back but she didn't show. I was tired so I locked up and went home."

"Nobody wants a quilt that bad." He snorted.

"You don't know quilters." I smirked.

"Tell your mom, thanks for the coffee." He rinsed his cup out and set it in the sink. He turned around and stared at me. "And Dove?"

"Let me guess." I narrowed my eyes.

"Stay out of this case." We spoke in unison.

I shook my head. "You need to hurry up and get it solved. I'm tired of the looks I get around town." I countered.

He gave me a long look but said nothing. I listened as his steps fell heavy on the wood floor.

After Dean left, I got busy quilting a Log Cabin Quilt. The customer had wanted it detailed so I knew it would take me longer to finish it. As I quilted, I let my mind wander over this whole murder.

Could Polly O'Hara have killed Gertrude? She

didn't seem like the type to go around hitting people in the head, but she had already admitted to slapping her. Did she have some help in committing the crime? Who would she know in Harland Creek that would help her?

The rest of the day passed uneventfully and at five o'clock, Mom poked her head into the room. "It's quitting time, Dove. I have dinner plans at Elizabeth's house. She told me to bring you along."

"Tell her next time. I have some things I want to research when I get back home."

"As long as you don't go anywhere by yourself." She gave me the look that let me know she was serious.

After I left the quilt shop, I dropped by the diner and grabbed a burger to go. I decided I needed to go out to the RV park and talk to Polly myself.

I drove out of Harland Creek toward the RV Park. It didn't take me long until I was pulling into the driveway of the establishment. I drove slowly down the lane, looking between old campers that looked like they were barely holding together. There was one Class A RV that was about twenty years old. I slowed down when the door opened. An old man who looked to be in his eighties climbed down the stairs with a beer in his hand. He went over to the grill beside the RV and began firing it up.

"That's not her." I kept driving. I had almost given up when I came to a newer looking Class A RV with a car parked in front.

I knew that car. That was the car that Polly O'Hara had squealed tires out of the parking lot.

I saw some movement in the window and decided to park away from the RV so I could watch her for a while.

I pulled over by an empty slot and held my breath as I killed the engine. The car backfired and spit out a column of smoke. I saw Polly in the RV pull the curtain to the side and peer out. Wide-eyed she scanned the park for someone with a gun. I finally breathed when the curtain fell back.

My stomach growled and I pulled my burger out of the bag. As I ate, I noticed the types of people who occupied the park.

There was an older couple who sat out under the awning of their campers in chairs and watched the squirrels in the trees as they chatted. They looked like they lived out of the camper and had been here for a while. There were quite a few campers with younger people hanging around, smoking and drinking and being loud. They looked like the kind of people that Winston hung around with.

I had finished my burger and was nursing my soda when Polly's RV door flew open. I sat up straight.

Polly looked to the right and then to the left before stepping outside. She hurried out to her car and unlocked it. She popped the trunk and got a plastic tote out. After making sure none of the nefarious males were headed toward her, she locked her car and headed back to the RV.

I slid out of my car, made sure my door was locked and started making my way to the RV. I spotted a Dodge Charger and froze.

Louie.

The car pulled up in front of Polly's RV.

I turned back to my car and slid inside, hoping he had not spotted me.

I hunched down in the seat and watched in horror as Louie got out of the car.

He glanced around, stuck a toothpick in his mouth and walked up to the RV. The door opened. Polly didn't look surprised to see him. She stepped aside and let him in.

"I wasn't expecting that." I slid out of my car to get a better look inside.

I walked over to the window, but it was too high up to see anything. I spotted a bucket by the firepit and grabbed it. After setting it under the window, I stepped onto it. It creaked under my weight but held.

I stretched up on my tiptoes to see inside.

Polly was shaking her head and looked distraught. Louie, in an uncharacteristic move, patted her on the shoulder as if he were comforting her.

I thought they didn't know each other. If Polly wanted to get back at Gertrude maybe she had hired Louie to have her killed. But why would she have Gertrude killed over rent? And why would Louie agree?

My mind and my heart raced a mile a minute as puzzle pieces began to twist inside my head.

MYSTERY OF THE TEA CUP QUILT

And then it happened.

The bucket creaked and suddenly my foot went through the bottom. I screamed and fell to the ground.

The door of the RV flew open and Louie and Polly rushed out.

All I could do was look up from my position on the ground.

"What the hell are you doing?" He scowled.

I pushed myself up on my elbows and scrambled to my feet. I tugged the bucket off my foot and tossed it to the side. "I just came by to see Polly." I dusted myself off as my heart raced.

"Looks like you were snooping." He snarled.

"I knocked but no one answered. I was just trying to see if Polly was home." Once again I lied.

"What do you want?" Polly glared.

I avoided his eyes and looked right at Polly. "That Tula Pink fabric you wanted came in. You can pick it up at your convenience." I forced a smile and headed to my car.

I didn't breathe as I walked those fifteen steps. Any moment I expected Louie to grab me from behind and haul me into the RV to end my life. Once I slid into my car, I locked the doors and started the engine. Thankfully the engine roared to life on the first try. I tried to act calm as I drove away, but once I hit the main road I broke the speed limit to get home.

CHAPTER 18

I called an emergency meeting of the Harland Creek Quilt Club that night. The ladies, along with Petunia, piled into Mom's living room and took a seat.

I looked at Elizabeth. "You couldn't leave Petunia home for one night?"

She lifted her chin. "Grayson took Heather out for dinner, and I didn't want her to stay at the house alone. Besides, she should be here. If it wasn't for her, you wouldn't have found out about that gravel deal with Wendy."

She had me there.

I glanced around the room and frowned. "Where's Weenie?"

"She said she had a previous engagement." Sylvia snorted. "I think she's got a boyfriend that she'd not told us about."

"Weenie?" I arched my eyebrow.

"She is the only one of us that has never been married. Maybe she wants a taste of that life." Bertha shrugged.

"So what's the emergency? Did Dean find the killer?" Agnes leaned back and studied me.

"Not that I know of. I found out something and I wanted to run it by you ladies before I talk to Dean."

"Go ahead, Dove." Mom sat on the edge of the chair and gave me her full attention.

"I went over to the RV Park to talk to Polly about the altercation she had with Gertrude."

"What happened?" Donna asked.

"I parked my car and was about to go up to the door when Louie pulled up in his Dodge Charger."

The ladies gasped.

Lorraine leaned forward in her seat. "Did he see you? Did you get out?"

"No. I stayed in my car and waited to see what he was going to do. Which turned out to be a good thing. He knocked on Polly's door and she let him in."

"She did?" Maggie gasped. "Why in the world would she ever open her door to that horrendous man?"

"I don't think she thinks he's as horrendous as we do. After he followed her inside, I snuck closer to the RV to see what was going on inside. The window was too tall and so I grabbed a bucket and turned it over. I stepped on it and peered through the window."

"Oh Dove, that was very foolish of you. They could have spotted you." Mom chastised.

"Hush, Mildred." Agnes waved her off. "Dove, what did you see?"

"They were talking and Polly looked upset, distressed. Louie appeared to be comforting her. They seemed…familiar with each other."

Another gasp went up around the room.

"Maybe they do know each other." Agnes nodded. "Maybe they got together and decided to kill Gertrude."

"What's the motive?" Elizabeth stroked Petunia's head. "I get that Louie would kill Gertrude to get the inheritance. But what about Polly? She wanted her money back from staying in that awful place and Gertrude stiffed her. But that's not motive enough for murder."

"I have a client who comes in every three months to get her hair permed and she lives out in one of those old campers." Sylvia shook her head. "Poor thing lives on a budget and can't come more often. Anyway, she said she heard the commotion between Gertrude and Polly. She said Gertrude threatened to tell the world that Polly doesn't write her own books. That's when Polly slapped her. As Gertrude stormed off, she said she was going to ruin Polly."

A slow smile grew on my face. "Ruining someone's career. Sounds like a pretty good motive to me. The only thing I don't understand is why would Polly and Louie go in together to commit murder. I mean they don't know each other."

"Or do they?" Donna cocked her head. "You know

how Louie has a Brooklyn accent. It's faded over time but it's still there. I noticed Polly had a hint of a Brooklyn accent, too. Maybe they do know each other."

I nodded. "It's certainly plausible."

Donna pulled out a notebook. "I copied our suspect list down so we can add to it." She pulled a pen out of her purse. "Here's what we have so far." She cleared her throat.

"Winston, AKA, Courthouse Steps. Motive. Winston finds out he was written out of the will. He goes to confront Gertrude and in a rage, he kills her.

Louie, AKA Monkey Wrench. Motive. Louie gains an inheritance from Gertrude's death. He follows her to the quilt shop, waits until she's inside and kills her.

Eleanor, AKA Drunkards Path. Eleanor knew Gertrude was blackmailing her with photos of her breaking into Sylvia and Maggie's building. She could have followed her and killed her in the quilt shop because she knew it would put the blame off her."

Donna looked up. "We haven't given Polly a quilt block name."

"How about Card Trick?" Bertha offered.

"No, it should be something related to her." Maggie frowned in concentration.

"How about House that Jack Built? She did mention she lost her house in the divorce and is living in an RV." I suggested.

"That's a good one, Dove." Donna smiled with satisfaction and wrote the new name in her notebook.

"Polly, AKA House That Jack Built. She's already on edge trying to get a book written…"

"Wait. If she really didn't write her own books, then why was she so stressed about being on deadline?" Agnes asked.

The room went silent for a minute.

"She said she was working on a new book, a cozy quilting series. Something totally off from what she normally wrote. What if she were actually writing this cozy series? She really is on deadline. Maybe Gertrude was talking about the romance books? Maybe Polly didn't write the romance books? Polly still gets royalties from her old books, so if people find out, they will stop buying and the money dries up." I looked around the room.

"Very good, Dove. You're better than Perry Mason." Sylvia winked.

Donna cleared her throat. "The next suspect is Wendy, AKA Pinwheel. She was already upset with Gertrude for stealing her antique furniture. Now she gets a gravel company wanting to lease her land and Gertrude gets wind of it. Gertrude wants the money. She tried to buy the land from Wendy. Wendy refuses and maybe Gertrude threatens her. That would be motive for killing."

"I'm not sure how strong a motive it is, though," Mom shook her head.

"You forgot one other suspect." Bertha stated.

"Who?" Donna frowned.

"Dove, AKA Dove in the window." Bertha cocked her head.

I sighed heavily.

"We're only putting real suspects down, Bertha." Agnes snarled.

"She is a real suspect. Dove and Gertrude were the only two who were in the building the night of the murder. And Dove is the only one left." Bertha narrowed her eyes at me. "Did you have a motive to kill Gertrude, Dove?"

"I will not have you talk to Dove like this." Mom stood up and glared at Bertha.

"I'm just wanting the facts. It's not personal, Mildred. You should know this." Bertha shrugged.

"Mom, it's okay." I swallowed hard. I looked around the room.

"We did have an argument. Gertrude wanted the quilt done that night. She was very insistent. I told her I was only human and could only do so much. She called me a few names. After that I made her leave." I left out the part where Gertrude threatened me. I just couldn't bring myself to tell my mom the truth about what had happened in New York.

"That's not a motive to kill." Donna insisted.

"But we still have to keep her name up there. Until the case is solved." Bertha narrowed her eyes on me.

"She's right. Leave it up there." I nodded. "Right now I feel like the strongest pair that have motive is Polly and Louie. I think we need to find a connection between them and then take it to Dean. Maybe he'll be more apt to believe us with some convincing evidence."

"You're right." Mom stood up. "I appreciate everyone coming and getting involved. Hopefully this thing will be solved within the next few days."

That night as I went to bed my mind ran wild. The list of suspects was starting to narrow, yet I still had a gut feeling I could not pinpoint who had committed the murder.

CHAPTER 19

I had just finished another quilt, a Jacob's Ladder, on the longarm machine, thankful I was making record time in getting the quilt orders done, when I spotted a late notice that had come in the mail that morning. I decided to ask Mom about it. She started to brush me off but finally told me she was a little behind on paying rent that month.

Guilt hit me hard. I had wanted to give my Mom a better life with my success, but in my foolish pride I had trusted someone I shouldn't have, and lost it all.

"Dove? Are you here?" Patricia called out.

I headed out into the store. "Hey Patricia. I didn't expect you back until next week."

Patricia stood at the register with the tote balanced on one ample hip. She jumped when I walked up.

She blushed. "I finished cutting these charm packets and wanted to get them back to Mildred. I know she needs all the business she can get. And these are selling like hot cakes." She set the tote down on the floor.

"Great! You got these done quickly. She will definitely be pleased." I looked over the stacks of charm packets, all cut in five in squares and tied neatly with a blue ribbon.

"It wasn't hard to do. It helps me get away from Mother." A sad expression crossed her face. "She is one of the most critical people I know. You're lucky, Dove. To have such an understanding mother."

I shifted my weight, not exactly sure how to respond. "I'm sure it's hard to care for your mom with all her health conditions. She's probably just depressed and taking it out on you."

Patricia shook her head slowly. "No, she's always been like that. Always telling me I needed to lose weight, or how no one will ever marry me. She even criticizes my quilting."

"Really? I just saw a quilt in the back that you did, and it's beautiful. Not many people can paper piece and that Medallion you did was gorgeous."

It was true. Patricia was a very talented quilter.

She lit up like a Christmas tree. "You really think so?"

"I know so. I wouldn't take your mom's words to heart. And as far as getting married, well, I think she's wrong, too."

Patricia looked hopeful for a second before her face fell. "She wasn't the only one who told me that."

I bristled. "Someone else said that to you?"

"Yes. Gertrude Brown. She was as mean as Mother." Patricia looked at the ground. "I hated to see her come into the store. She was always calling me fat and stupid."

My neck prickled. "She did? When?"

Patricia's face went red. "It doesn't matter. It's probably the truth."

"No, it's not. You need to start believing in yourself and stop listening to other people." I lifted my head. "You'll get married when you meet the right guy."

She smiled and relief spread across her face. "Is there anything else your mom needs me to do from home? Any quilt kits she needs put together?"

"I'm not sure. She had to run to the bank, but I'll have her call you. If she has something else for you to do, I'll run it by after work."

"Thanks, Dove. I appreciate it." She gave me a grateful smile and headed out the door.

I had no idea Gertrude had said those things to Patricia. It was cruel, for sure.

A police car pulled up to the front door. I watched with interest as Dean and Tarzan stepped out of the car.

I stepped back so he could open the door.

"You can't bring a dog in here." I pointed to Tarzan who seemed to narrow his eyes on me.

"It's almost ninety degrees outside. I'm not leaving him in the car," Dean stepped inside with the dog and commanded the beast to sit. "Besides, I know you allow Petunia in here."

I lifted my chin. "That's different."

"Right. She's a goat. A lot dirtier than a dog."

I narrowed my eyes. "She is not dirty."

"I'm not here to discuss animals. I'm here to go over the suspects with you."

My heart leaped in my chest. I smiled. "You're actually updating me? Wow, that's a big step for you."

He walked over to the door and turned the sign to Closed and locked the door. "Come on. Let's go to the back of the room."

I followed him as he and Tarzan went into the classroom where Mom taught. I glanced at the list of suspects which we had named quilt blocks and smiled to myself.

He glanced at the white board, frowned, and then turned his attention back to me

"We're voting on which quilt to do next. I'm pulling for Drunkards Path, myself," I fibbed, trying desperately to keep any sign of it from my face.

He leaned against the table set up in front of the room and crossed his arms over his chest

"Did you know we got a tip from the RV park that Louie was seen in the RV of Polly O'Hara?" He cut his eyes at me and watched my reaction.

"Really? How interesting." I tried to act nonchalant.

"Dove, the police track calls. I know that you are the one who called in that tip." He ran his hand through his hair.

I glared. "I had to. You won't listen to me otherwise." I plopped down in one of the plastic chairs and crossed my arms over my chest. "Don't you find it a little bit suspicious that an author who has no ties to this town, arrives a few days before a murder takes place? And that she had strong ties to Louie who had a strong motive to kill Gertrude?"

He stared at me for a beat. "I'll keep that in mind. In the meantime, I'm going to follow up on that pill you found and wondered if you wanted to go with me."

"Really?" I straightened.

"I figure if you're with me, you're less likely to get into trouble."

I bit my lip to keep from grinning. "Okay, but let me tell Mom that I have to leave for a while."

As I sent my Mom a quick text, I prayed that this lead would prove successful.

CHAPTER 20

I grabbed my purse, followed Dean outside, and watched as he loaded Tarzan into the back of his car. He turned, looking at me. "Well, are you coming or what?"

"Are you sure it's safe for me to get in that car? With him?" I swipe a bead of sweat off my brow and stared at Tarzan.

"Yes, now will you hurry up?" He didn't wait for me but slid into the driver's seat.

I screwed up my courage and went over to the passenger's side and got in. Thankfully, Dean had the air conditioner turned up high, making the inside of the car a bit more tolerable.

He backed up and drove out of the parking lot.

I looked over at him. "What do you know about Louie? Does he have a police record? I heard he breaks into people's houses when they aren't home."

He jerked his head in my direction. "Whose home?"

"I can't say. But the woman was terrified to find him in her kitchen."

Dean ran his hand through his hair. "People are intimidated by Louie. I've run his name and tried to find any criminal record but he comes up clean."

"What about Gertrude? Did she have a criminal record? I heard she was quite the troublemaker in Harland Creek before she died. Theft. Dog fighting ring. Fleecing customers from her RV Park. Blackmail."

"The dog fighting was before I became Chief of Police. And Gertrude paid off the previous chief to look the other way. After I got the position, Gertrude had intimidated so many people with Louie, that people refused to press charges. I'm hoping to change that."

"I hope you do, too." I meant it. "As much as I love a field trip, I have to ask. Where are we going?"

"Remember that pill you found in the quilt shop?"

"Yes." My heart sped up.

"I had it tested and it's not a narcotic." He glanced at me as he drove.

I was disappointed. If it wasn't an illegal substance, then that would rule Winston out. "So what is it?"

"It's some type of medicine. We are headed to the pharmacy where a friend of mine has sent it off to be tested."

"Does the police department not have its own testing?"

"We're a small town, Dove. If I sent it off, it would

have to go to the state lab and it would take weeks to get a result. This way is faster."

I nodded, glad that he wanted quick results.

We pulled up in front of Thornton's Pharmacy off the town square. I frowned. "Thornton's has a lab? The last time I was in here, it barely carried the basics."

"The new owner updated a lot of things when she bought it. She has connections to a chemist at Mississippi State University. She said she could tell me what kind of pill it is."

"Perfect." I followed him out of the car. Tarzan was at his side.

"Hey Dean. Hey Tarzan. Want the usual?" An older gentleman was behind the diner counter and gave us all smiles.

"No thanks, Mills. We are here to see the pharmacist." Dean nodded at Tarzan. "But I think Tarzan would like a puppy cone if you don't mind."

"Coming right up." Mills turned his attention to making a miniature ice cream cone for the German Shepherd who sat when Dean commanded. "Go on back, Dean. She's waiting for you."

"You must be a frequent customer if he knows what you like so much." I snorted.

"Grabbing dinner here is quick and easy. That way I don't have to fool with cooking when I get home." He walked to the room in the back and stopped at a room labeled Private. "It's through here."

I waved him ahead of me. "Lead the way."

He stepped into the room which looked more like a

mad scientist's laboratory than a pharmacy. "You would think your friend could identify the pill with all this equipment instead of sending it off." I picked up a white bottle and shook it.

"Put that down." Dean frowned.

"Dean, you're here." A beautiful woman in a white lab jacket came around the corner and launched herself at him. She hugged him tight and kissed his cheek.

"Hello, Samantha." He gave me a nervous look. "This is Dove Agnew. Mildred's daughter."

My stomach dropped. Samantha Vaughn. Holy crap. It was the woman from his Facebook picture. The one he'd spend a night with under the stars.

She was even more beautiful in person.

I forced a smile and stepped forward. "Hi, nice to meet you." I didn't want this woman to know how much it bothered me to see her with him.

"Dove, so nice to meet you. Mildred is such a sweet lady. She made me a quilt as a welcome gift to Harland Creek." Samantha came over and pulled me into a hug. I cringed. I wasn't much of a hugger by any means, and certainly wasn't into hugging my ex-boyfriend's girlfriend.

"That sounds just like Mom." I laughed nervously. "So Dean says you can tell us what kind of pill was found."

She blinked as if remembering we were here for a reason and not a social call.

I immediately did not like Samantha Vaughn. Not at all.

"Samantha, did you know Gertrude Brown?" I cocked my head.

"She came in to get her blood pressure medication once a month. That's usually the only time I saw her." Samantha shrugged. "Although I am sorry to hear about her death."

"How were your interactions with Gertrude?" I pressed. Maybe the killer was standing in front of me. That would certainly be convenient for me. Wrapping up a murder case and putting an end to the little romance between these two.

"Dove." Dean warned.

"Fine." I sighed.

"What did you find out about the pill?" Dean looked at Samantha.

"Well, like I said it wasn't a narcotic. Nor was it a pain pill of any kind. It was a diuretic pill."

"To make you pee?" I frowned.

"Exactly." Samantha looked pleased that I understood the medical lingo.

"And what kinds of reasons would someone take a diuretic pill?" I wracked my head thinking over the list of suspects.

"Well, there are lots of reasons. Blood pressure, edema or swelling in the legs, or heart failure." She looked from me to Dean. "I should be getting back exactly which kind of diuretic it was from my chemist friend in a few days."

Dean sighed. "I see. So all the disorders you named off could be tied to any one of the people that shop in the quilt shop." He looked at me. "Dove, isn't your mom on high blood pressure medicine? Maybe it's her pill. And I know that Bertha and Weenie both have issues with their legs. Maybe it belongs to one of them?"

"My mom doesn't bring her medicines to work. She takes them before she leaves home. And as for Weenie and Bertha, it's their feet they have issues with. Not their legs. I know for a fact both of them can outrun me in the dark." I lifted my chin.

He narrowed his eyes at me. "Thank you Samantha for all your help, but we have to get going." He grabbed my elbow and ushered me out the door.

"Tarzan, let's go." He didn't stop walking until we were all out the door and standing on the sidewalk. He let go of me and parked his hands on his hips. "We had a report a few nights ago about someone breaking and entering Gertrude's house. At night. The person that called in said she swore she saw a bunch of old women in a van speeding away. Tell me that wasn't you and your mom's quilting buddies."

I blinked.

"Dove, answer me."

"You told me not to tell you, so I figured I would just stay silent on this one."

He let out a curse. "You could have been in danger. You can't go around breaking into people's homes."

"I didn't break in. The door was unlocked. And second, I bet the person that called the cops was Wendy Rutherford." I looked at him but he said nothing.

A slow smile grew across my face. "Did you ask her what she was doing in Gertrude's house?"

"I did. She said she saw someone with lights bobbing around inside and figured someone was trying to break in. She went in to look and saw two older women hobbling away and someone wearing a glow-in-the-dark T-shirt. Said the fabric had a bone on it."

My smile faded. He glanced down at my T-shirt. Today I was wearing a yellow T-shirt with a giraffe wearing glasses and the words "What's Up?'

I'd quit reading the T-shirts I was wearing. I figured it didn't matter and it wasn't like I had any better options.

My eyes widened. "It doesn't glow. I swear."

"Get in the car and I'll drive you back to the shop." He opened the passenger's side door and waited for me.

"What about the pill? What if it belongs to the killer?"

"Unless Winston or Louie has heart failure or edema, then you're wrong. It's not a clue. It belongs to one of the old women who frequent the shop." He glared until I got into the car.

As we drove back to the quilt shop, I sat in silence.

Maybe Dean was right. Maybe it wasn't a clue. All I knew was there were still suspects, and I was going to find the killer, no matter what.

CHAPTER 21

*O*nce Dean dropped me off at the quilt shop, I went back inside. Elizabeth Harland was there looking at some fabric with Petunia in tow. Mom was busy helping two customers so I slipped back into the back room where the whiteboard was located.

I studied the board. "I wonder if Gertrude had any health issues? Maybe it's her pill and the tablet fell out of her purse when she was hit in the head. If it is hers, then I can rule the pill out as a clue to the killer."

I realized the only way I was going to find out if Gertrude was taking a diuretic pill was to go back to the pharmacy and ask Samantha.

I cringed. Samantha was the last person I wanted to talk to. Besides, I'm sure there were privacy laws regarding patient medication.

The only other option was to head over to Gertrude's house and look for a pill bottle myself.

I poked my head out of the room. "Mom, can you spare me for a minute?"

She smiled and nodded. "Yes, Patricia is headed over to pick up some quilt fabric to cut up fat quarters. And Donna said she was going to stop by after lunch. Where are you going?"

"I need to check on something."

Mom excused herself from the customers and walked over to me. "Dove Agnew, you better not be putting yourself in danger."

"Mom, I'm not a little kid anymore." I huffed.

"And you're not going anywhere by yourself." She glared.

Elizabeth walked over. "Why don't you take Petunia with you?"

"Take a goat?"

"Yes. She seems to be proving herself useful with this case." Elizabeth lifted her chin proudly.

I looked at my mom. "If I take the goat, will you stop worrying?"

"I won't worry as much." Mom smiled. "Besides, how much trouble can you get into with a goat in tow?"

"Fine. Give me her leash. I won't be long." I grabbed my keys and headed to my car. I put Petunia in the backseat, but she jumped into the passenger's seat before I could get in.

"Don't eat anything. This car is barely holding together as it is." I glared. I pulled out of the driveway and headed towards Gertrude's house.

When I turned onto her road, I passed Wendy's house. I noticed her car was gone. Maybe she'd stay gone long enough for me to have a look around Gertrude's house without her calling the cops.

I didn't pull into Gertrude's driveway but parked off the road, in case I needed to make a quick getaway. Once again my car backfired, sending up a smoke signal into the sky.

So much for being stealthy.

I made my way with Petunia in tow, up the driveway to the front door. It took longer than expected since she wanted to chew every blade of grass and weed we came across.

There was no vehicle in the driveway, and I was hoping to get in and out before anyone saw me.

I tried the front door but it was locked. I didn't have my lock-picking tool, so I decided to go around back to check the backdoor.

I tried the doorknob but it was locked as well.

I looked at Petunia who was chewing on an overgrown shrub by the door. "Now what do we do?"

She looked up at me with her goat eyes and let out a bleat.

I frowned. "Sorry, I don't speak goat."

Petunia tugged out of my grip and ran.

"Stop! Don't you dare run off!" I gave her a stern look

She stopped under the window I had climbed out of and looked up at it.

"Oh, good idea."

After I grabbed her leash, I tied it to a tree. I looked at the window and tried pushing it up. Slowly it came up until there was room enough for me to squeeze in.

"Stay here and don't run off." I looked at Petunia.

I climbed through the window, stood and dusted off my shirt, then looked around. Weenie's box, which I'd dropped on the bed ,was gone. I poked my head out the window to make sure Petunia was still there. She was contentedly chewing on a clump of wild flowers growing around the tree.

I headed into the kitchen and began going through cabinets. I stopped when I spotted a shelf with multiple prescription bottles

I picked them up and read the labels. One was an antibiotic and the other was medicine for high blood pressure. There were no prescriptions for any pain medication or diuretic.

I heard someone at the front door and the door knob rattle. "Crap." I ran down the hallway to the bedroom, glancing behind me. A figure dressed in black came running after me. I slammed the bedroom door closed and locked it.

"Hey, what are you doing in here? When I get my hands on you, you're going to wish you never meddled in my business, lady. And I won't stop there. I'll get your family, too." Louie called out from the other side of the door.

My blood ran cold. I grabbed the chest of drawers and shoved it against the door to buy me some time to make a get-away. I scrambled out of the window and struggled to untie Petunia's leash. I heard the back door slam shut.

Louie was outside with his large hands clenched into fists. "You realized I could end you right now?"

We locked eyes for a second before Petunia let out a bleat and broke free of her leash. She ran for the tree line. I followed on the goat's hooves.

We made it to the tree line with Louie running after us. I spotted an area of overgrown foliage and grabbed Petunia. She let out a single bleat as I ran into the cover of the woods.

My heart thumped in my chest as I ran as fast as I could. Suddenly, I barreled into someone.

We both crumpled to the ground in a heap.

Petunia bleated and I quickly covered her mouth. My mouth dropped open as I looked at the person I had run into.

Wendy Rutherford.

She looked as scared as I did.

We heard approaching footsteps, and she pressed her finger to her lips in a gesture of remaining silent. I squatted down, praying there were no poison ivy leaves near us. Petunia, still in my arms, looked up at me. She started to wiggle as I heard approaching footsteps. Wendy grabbed a white flower and stuck it near her mouth to keep her quiet. She happily chewed.

The footsteps went further away from us until I knew Louie was gone.

"What are you doing here?" Wendy frowned as she stood up and dusted herself off.

"I could ask you the same." I slowly stood.

"I was trying to get my furniture back. The items that Gertrude stole." She glared. "I heard someone come through a window and I ran out to hide until they were gone." She arched her eyebrow. "I should have known you'd break in again."

I narrowed my eyes. "You were the one that called the cops the other night."

"Yes. I thought you were breaking in to steal my furniture."

I blinked. "Why don't you get more furniture? I know about the contract that the gravel company is offering."

She blinked. "And I guess you know I turned the deal down."

My mouth dropped open. "You what? But I thought.."

"You thought I could be bought." Wendy lifted her chin. "I inherited the house from my aunt after her death. I used to come visit her in the summers, when my parents shipped me off so they could travel the world. I've lived a life of luxury, Dove. Now I want to live a life that counts. I want my furniture back because it comes with memories."

"But I thought…."

"You thought I killed Gertrude so I could get her land and lease it to the gravel company." Wendy gave me a sad look. "It was Gertrude that wanted to buy my land. She wanted the gravel contract. I refused. After that, she stole my furniture and I was too scared to say anything. She had a habit of keeping a list of people's secrets just in case she needed to blackmail them." She shook her head.

"I'm sorry. I didn't know." Guilt tugged deep in my stomach. I knew then, that Wendy couldn't be the murderer.

"Of course, you didn't know. You didn't bother to ask." She sighed heavily. "Go home, Dove." Wendy gave me one last look and headed in the direction of her house.

I wasn't sure how long I stood there with Petunia in my arms. I felt really bad about accusing Wendy of murder. And she was right about one thing. Gertrude did keep a list of people's secrets. She was the cruelest human I'd ever come across.

I heard a twig snap. Fear crawled up my spine. I tightened my grip on the goat and hurried back to my car with Petunia in my arms and terror in my heart.

I stayed at the quilt shop with Petunia until closing time. Elizabeth had called and said she was running late.

I didn't mind babysitting the goat a little longer. Since our dangerous adventure, she was curled up in the corner of the room taking a nap, worn out from our brush with death.

The run in with Louie had me on edge. Every time Mom would drop her pen or slam the door, I would jump. I kept getting up and going to the window to make sure Louie was not waiting outside for me.

"Dove, what is going on with you? You are as nervous as a long-tail cat in a room full of rocking chairs."

"Sorry. Just have a lot on my mind." I filled up my coffee cup and looked at Mom. "What are you doing tonight?" I hope she didn't have another dinner planned with her friends. She needed to be at home where I could keep my eye on her.

"Oh, I thought I'd stay late to get some more quilts done."

I froze. "By yourself? Can't you work on them tomorrow?"

"I was hoping to get caught up." Mom gave me a smile. "While you were out, I had new locks put on the door. So I'm safe."

"Not if the killer can pick the lock." I reminded her. "I don't like you being here by yourself. I'm going to stay with you. That way we can get caught up on some work."

"Patricia, called while you were out. I mentioned to her about staying late. She said she could come help with the quilts after dark, once her mother goes to sleep. She feels like whoever sent that letter won't be watching the store at night."

"She may be company but certainly not someone who could help protect you. She doesn't need to come. I'll stay."

"Honey, you can't control everything."

"You're not talking me out of this. I'm staying. I'll call Patricia and tell her there's no need for her to come." I turned on my heel to check to see the door was locked and that Louie wasn't going to make good on his promise.

CHAPTER 22

A knock on the door of the quilt shop made me nearly jump out of my skin. With my heart in my throat, I peered around the corner and saw Dean standing at the door.

"Who is it?" Mom called out from her sewing machine.

"Dean. I'll see what he wants." I calmed my racing heart and moved toward the door.

I flipped the lock and opened the door. I moved to allow him entrance. "What are you doing here? You nearly gave me a heart attack."

He stepped inside, glancing around. "Saw lights on as I drove by. I thought I would stop to make sure everything was okay."

"We are just staying late, trying to finish some work."

He nodded slowly. "Just you and your mom here?"

"No. Petunia is here, too." Right on cue, Petunia

walked out of Mom's office, heading straight for the Tula Pink fabric we'd gotten in a few days ago.

I grabbed her collar. "Don't you dare eat that fabric."

He shook his head.

"Is that all you wanted? You didn't stop by to let me know you caught the killer?" I lifted my chin defiantly.

He narrowed his gaze. "Actually, I came by to tell you if you break into Gertrude's house again you will be arrested."

My smile slipped. "You talked to Louie."

He nodded once.

"Did he tell you he threatened to harm me?"

"He said he threatened you to get you off his property." He cocked his head and studied me.

"Wait, his property?" I frowned. "I thought the will hadn't been read yet."

"It was read this afternoon. And it confirmed that Louie inherits everything."

"Motive to kill. Dean, it's right there in front of your face."

"I have no evidence." His expression was grim.

"When Louie talked to you did he also tell you he threatened my mother as well?"

He jerked his head towards me. "No, he didn't. What exactly did he say?"

"He said that I was going to wish I had never meddled in his business. And he won't stop there. He said that he was going to get my family, too." I glared. "Did he tell you that?"

"No. Looks like I need to have a talk with Louie." He

turned to leave and stopped. "You want me to post a police officer outside the store while you and your mom are here?"

I nodded. "That would be nice." I smiled, grateful for the offer.

He nodded and put his hand on the door handle. "I'll make the call. And Dove, keep the door locked."

I watched as he made his way to his car. He looked intently at me as he climbed into the front seat. I could tell he was upset. Probably because I had committed a crime by breaking into Gertrude's house. Maybe he was upset because he was tired of me meddling. But some part of me thought he was worried for my safety, and that made me feel a little warm around my heart.

I reached for the lock just as Elizabeth drove up. She eased out of her truck and gave me a wave. Petunia spotted her and ran between my legs out the door.

"Petunia, be careful." I darted out after the little goat.

She ran straight to Elizabeth and began jumping up and down, like an excited child.

"Hey, sweet girl." Elizabeth rubbed the goat's head and smiled. "You miss Gammy?"

"Gammy?" It was the first time I heard Elizabeth refer to herself as a grandmother to a goat.

She blushed and grinned. "Yes, Gammy. I've grown to love this little goat as if she were one of my grandkids. You probably think I'm crazy."

I smiled. "I think it's cute."

Petunia came over and looked up at me. I rubbed her head. "You're pretty smart for a goat, aren't you?"

Petunia let out a bleat.

"I brought you and your mom something to eat. I didn't know if you two had a chance to eat."

"We missed dinner. Thanks for thinking of us. That's awfully nice of you." My stomach rumbled as if on cue

She went around to the passenger's side and opened the door. "I put everything in these casserole carriers to keep things warm. It's fried chicken, creamed corn, mashed potatoes, gravy and homemade biscuits." She held out the containers.

"Wow, that's great. And very much appreciated. Thank you Elizabeth."

"Anytime, Dove. Call if you or Mildred need anything." She patted the passenger's side seat and Petunia jumped up in the truck.

"I will. Thanks again." I watched as she drove away before heading inside.

I got the door opened just as a scream tore through the shop.

It came from my mom.

My blood went cold in my veins. I threw the casserole carriers onto the counter and ran back to the back room. A large figure dressed in black and wearing a ski mask ran towards me.

My heart stuttered and I froze to where I was standing.

The figure came barreling into me, knocking me to

the ground. The dark stranger fell on top of me snarling and growling. The figure knocked the breath out of me. I struggled to breathe.

The attacker rolled off of me and ran out the door.

I scrambled to my feet and raced to the back room where my mom was.

Mom was on her knees cradling her head in her hands.

I knelt beside her. "Mom, are you okay?" I looked her over for any signs of blood but didn't see anything.

"I think so. " She pulled her hands away from her head.

I noticed a small knot rising on her head. "I'm calling 911."

I made the quick call and heard sirens almost immediately heading in our direction.

"Tell me exactly what happened." I held Mom's hand as we waited for help.

"I was going into the back room to get some coffee. That's when I spotted someone hiding in the corner. The person was dressed all in black and had that ski mask on. The intruder growled and ran towards me. It scared me so I turned to run. That's when the awful individual hit me."

"You don't know who it was? Recognize the voice?"

"No, I didn't. All he said was 'I told you to stay out of my business'."

My heart stumbled. "Louie." He'd told me the same thing.

The police ran inside the quilt shop to check everything out. Dean was the second man inside the shop. He knelt down beside my mom.

"Louie, he did this." I looked at him.

Dean looked at Mom. "Is that true?"

She frowned and blinked. "You know, I'm not sure. But I don't think it was Louie."

"Why not?" I asked.

"Because this person wasn't as tall as Louie."

I thought about Mom's words as the paramedics loaded her up in the ambulance to take her to the ER to have a CT of her head.

If it wasn't Louie? Then who?

Fear turned to anger in my gut.

It was one thing to try to hurt me, but quite another to hurt my mother.

If I hadn't been determined to take down Louie before, I was solid in my convictions now.

CHAPTER 23

I overslept the next morning and was late opening the store. I stayed at the hospital with Mom until her CT came back. The test came back clear. It was late and the doctor wanted her to stay overnight just for observation. She tried to argue but I agreed with the doctor.

The hospital would be the safest place for her. She would be watched constantly and the killer wouldn't dare harm her in there.

I got home around three in the morning and finally fell asleep. When I woke at eight, the first thing I did was call the hospital to check on mom. The nurse assured me she was fine and still sleeping. They said the doctor would probably release her around noon.

I pulled up to the shop and noticed a lot of cars in the parking lot. People were gathered around the front door, and Dean was standing there trying to calm people down.

I slid out of my car and hurried up the steps. "What's going on?"

"There she is. She tried to harm her own mother." A woman I recognized, but couldn't remember her name spoke up.

"Shut up, Carol. You don't know what you are talking about." Agnes Jackson scowled.

"Dove, saved Mildred." Elizabeth called out. "Anyone who says any different will have me to deal with."

God bless the Harland Creek Quilters. They would defend me to the end.

"Everyone calm down. I'm asking everyone to disperse this instant." Dean yelled.

Eleanor pushed her way to the front of the crowd. "Dean, you're not taking this case seriously. You still have emotional ties to Dove. You may even still love her. That's why you haven't arrested her yet."

"That's not true. He hasn't arrested me because I didn't do anything."

"Oh yeah?" She arched a brow plucked within an inch of its life. "How about this? You thought no one would find out what you did in New York. Well, missy, the chickens have come home to roost." She held up a New York paper with my face splattered across it. The headline read, 'Owner of Lady Catherine LeCroix designer of children's clothing named a suspect in smuggling drugs in clothing.'

I wanted to throw up. I pressed my hand over my heart to keep it from jumping out of my chest.

"Lady Catherine LeCroix? My grandchildren wear that line." Elizabeth frowned. "Dove, are you Lady Catherine LeCroix?"

"I...I.." I tried to speak but the words didn't come out.

Everyone went silent. Their hard stares felt like fire on me, judging and condemning me at the same time.

"Dove?" Donna stepped forward, looking at me.

Hot tears grew behind my eyes and I had to get away. I shoved through the crowd and unlocked the door as they bombarded me with questions. After opening the door, I locked it behind me.

I went into the backroom where we kept the quilts and slid down the wall. I sobbed as I pressed my head between my knees.

They knew. Everyone knew. I would never live this down.

"Dove."

I squeezed my eyes tight at the sound of Dean's voice. He was the last person I wanted to talk to .

"Go away."

"You lied." I could hear the hurt in his voice.

"You don't understand." How could he? He never wanted more than what he had. He never had dreams or aspirations. He was content in the town he was born in.

Silence stretched between us.

I heard him turn and head to the door.

I wept as his boots slowly walked away.

Once again, Dean had not believed in me.

"Dove?"

I jumped at the sound of Weenie's voice. I jerked my head up.

"Weenie, how did you get in here?"

"Dean forgot to lock the door when he left. Don't worry. Everyone is gone and I locked it behind me." Weenie pulled up a chair and sat in front of me.

"Why are you here, Weenie?" I looked up at her.

"I figured you wanted to tell your side of the story. I know what it feels like when people don't let you talk." She shrugged.

I smiled.

"Did you smuggle drugs?" She asked brightly.

Her expression made me laugh. "No. I didn't."

"Well, that's good." She smiled hopefully.

I dried my eyes. "I started the children's line under Catherine LeCroix. I never really liked my name. Kids made fun of it all the time."

"I know how you feel." Her voice was quiet yet sincere.

I nodded. "I bet you do, Weenie."

She didn't press me but let me take my time. "I didn't tell mom about my business because I wanted to wait until it was very successful. It started growing and I couldn't believe my luck. I soon took on a business partner named Cal Raport, who convinced me to change my manufacturer and distributor. He said I would make three times more money. And I did. What I didn't realize was he was smuggling drugs in the hems of my dresses. Apparently my partner had gotten a tip about a raid on the warehouse. He took all my money and went on the run. Leaving me holding the bag, and without a cent to my name."

"At least they didn't arrest you for it." Weenie blinked.

"Well, they interrogated me and had an investigation. They found out my partner had lied to me and I was not at fault. That's why I didn't get charged. They told me to make sure to keep out of trouble until they catch Cal. "

"So everything turned out alright."

"No, Weenie, it didn't." I shook my head. "I was going to sell the business and pay off any bills my mom had. I had enough money for her to retire and live comfortably for the rest of her life. Now, she's barely staying afloat and there's been a murder in her quilt shop, which isn't good for business."

Weenie nodded and grew thoughtful. "Dove, why didn't you tell your mom about your business? She told all of us you were a buyer at Nordstrom."

"I wanted to wait until I was successful. I wanted her to be proud."

"Dove, she's always been proud of you." Weenie gave me a smile so sincere it made me want to cry.

Tears welled up in my eyes again. "Thanks, Weenie."

"Weenie isn't my real name, you know."

"It isn't?"

"No. I was born on October 31. My mom named me Halloween. She shortened it to Weenie."

I blinked. "I see."

Weenie gave me a sad smile. "My mom was an alcoholic. The doctor said she was drunk when she went into labor. My grandmother practically raised me. You're lucky, Dove. You have a good mother."

I sniffed and wiped my eyes. "I know."

"So, looks like we need to solve this mystery and get back to quilting."

I looked at Weenie and smiled. "You're right." I stood up and gave her a hug. She was so tiny I was afraid I'd break her.

"Will you mind staying here and watching the store? I'm afraid the other ladies in the quilt group aren't going to want to help anymore."

"Of course, honey." She pulled something out of her purse. "I brought my mace just in case there's trouble. Oh and Dove, I don't think Winston is the killer. I saw him at the cemetery crying over Gertrude's grave. He kept saying, "Why did you leave me? Now I have no one. Made me feel bad for the guy."

"You're right. I don't think it's him either. And I have ruled out Wendy. But I know who it is." I gathered myself together and headed for my car.

Propelled by frustration and anger, I was going to find Louie and confront him once and for all.

CHAPTER 24

I cranked up the radio in the old Ford Taurus as I drove in the direction of where I knew the killer would be.

I tried building up my courage to confront the suspect. I had tried calling Dean, but it went straight to voicemail. I had a feeling he was ignoring me and my sleuthing skills.

By the time I pulled up in front of Polly O'Hara's RV, I was determined to get this case settled, once and for all.

My car backfired and sent up a plume of smoke. Polly threw open the door and stared outside, as if she were expecting to witness an explosion.

"It's you," she narrowed her eyes. She tried to shut the door, but I was quick and stuck in my foot.

"Yes, it's me," I gritted out between my teeth. "I'm coming inside whether you like it or not." I stepped inside, closing the door behind me.

"I'm calling the police." She reached for her cell phone.

"Please do. It will save me the trouble of calling. I want you to know that despite you and Louie's attack on my mom, she's going to be fine."

The blood drained from her face. "Attack? What attack?"

"Stop lying for him. Last night my mom was attacked and hit in the head."

Polly's eyes widened as she gasped. "Oh my. I had no idea."

"Either you start talking or I'm calling the cops myself to come arrest you.'

She shook her head violently. "No, don't. Look, I didn't have anything to do with the attack on your mom."

I arched my brow in disbelief. "What about Gertrude? I saw how cozy you and Louie were together. Don't bother lying about not knowing him."

Her shoulders slumped in defeat. "That is true. I do know Louie. We both lived in New Jersey."

I crossed my arms over my chest and glared at her.

She slumped into her recliner. "Sit down and I'll tell you everything."

I sat on the kitchen chair to face her, waiting for her to spill her guts.

"My husband, John, and Louie were business partners. They owned a construction business. Louie and his wife, Theresa, would often spend weekends at our house. We were all very close." She wrung her hands.

"One day I came home early from an author conference to find John and Theresa in bed together." Her voice cracked with emotion.

"I'm sorry. That must have been hard." I offered.

"I was devastated." She blinked back tears. "Anyway, I was so mad, I told Louie. He found John and beat him up. He was in the hospital for a week."

I frowned. "Did Louie get arrested?"

"John pressed charges. When he got out of the hospital, he served me with divorce papers. He moved Theresa into our home and I got the RV. I went into a deep depression and couldn't write. That's why I have so many deadlines. I got a call from Louie, and he told me to come down here to get away from things in New York. He said I'd be able to concentrate and get a lot written."

"That still doesn't explain what you and Gertrude were arguing about when you slapped her."

Polly blew out a breath. "She found out about my divorce and how John married Theresa and got the house. She also intercepted a certified letter that was dropped off here for me. It was confidential but she opened it. She said she knew I was using a ghostwriter for my books."

"Do you? Use a ghostwriter?" I cocked my head.

"No! But I was so far behind on deadlines that I contacted someone off a website. I was debating using her to write the romance book while I work on this cozy mystery."

"So Gertrude tried to blackmail you with that bit of information?"

"Yes. But it didn't matter that she knew. I ended up not using a ghostwriter and just calling my publisher and telling her the truth. About my depression, how behind I was, and asking for more time."

I frowned. "Then you didn't have a reason to kill Gertrude."

"No. I didn't."

"What were you looking so upset about when Louie came over?"

"I told him that if I didn't get this book written then I was going to end up losing my contract with my publisher. He was trying to give me a pep talk. He said that he believed in me and that I could get the book written in a week if I really tried." She brightened a little. "And since then, I've been writing like mad. I've not left the RV park and have written through the night." Her eyes met mine. "Louie may be rough around the edges, but he's been through a lot and can be someone good to have on your side in a pinch."

I studied Polly. Maybe they hadn't committed the crime together. She certainly didn't appear to be a hardened criminal but Louie was entirely different.

"You said John pressed charges against Louie. Did Louie ever go to jail?"

"Why don't you ask me yourself?"

I spun around in my seat to see Louie standing in the doorway.

I slowly stood. "Louie."

He narrowed his eyes. "Looks like you're still sticking your nose in other people's business."

"It becomes my business when my mother gets attacked in her own place of business."

Louie didn't blink an eye at that piece of information.

"Louie, Dove was just asking how we knew each other." Polly stood and went to the refrigerator. She pulled out a bottle of water. "Anyone want something to drink?"

"No thanks." I kept my eyes on Louie. "Is that right? You and Polly know each other from New Jersey?"

"Yes. I was business partners with John." His eyes hardened at the mention of his former friend and business partner.

"Louie, where were you last night?" I swallowed hard as I waited for his answer.

"Just tell her, Louie. It doesn't matter." Polly sighed heavily.

Louie stayed silent.

"Oh, for goodness sake. Louie was here with me." Polly shook her head. "I will never understand why you are so tightlipped about everything, Louie."

"The whole night?" I arched a brow.

Louie stared at me as a slight grin played at his lips.

I looked at Polly. Her face went red. "Yes. Louie was here all night."

"I see. So he has an alibi." I nodded and made my

way to the door. I turned. "Thank you for telling me the truth, Polly. I hope you get your book written. I know a lot of quilters who would love to read it."

She gave me a genuine smile.

CHAPTER 25

I stepped outside Polly's RV and scanned the campgrounds. I spotted the same couple I saw every time I drove through sitting out under the awning of their camper.

I made my way over to them and smiled.

"Excuse me, I hope I'm not disturbing you." I smiled.

"We ain't buying nothing. And we are already are saved." The old man with a plaid short sleeved shirt and jeans swatted at a fly from his position in his folding chair. The old woman sitting beside him wore a pink T-shirt with a Bible verse and cut off jean shorts. She sipped on something that looked like sweet tea from a red Solo cup.

I blinked. "Well, that's good to hear. I'm just needing some information."

The old man barked out a laugh. "My name is Earl and this is Wellsy."

"Nice to meet you both." I smiled.

"Want some sweet tea, honey?" Wellsy asked.

"No, thank you. I was wondering if you happened to see that Dodge Charger parked out in front of Polly O'Hara's RV last night." I jerked my thumb over my shoulder to the RV.

"Why, yes I did." Wellsy nodded. "It arrived around six p.m. I know because that's when we grill out."

"Did you see when it left?"

Wellsy smiled. "It pulled out of here around seven this morning."

"But you don't know if the vehicle was there all night? I mean the owner could have left late, like around midnight, and come back around two in the morning." It was plausible that Louie left and came back after the attack.

"Oh, that's impossible." Wellsy laughed.

"How is that impossible?" I frowned.

"Because I have trouble sleeping. I read a lot and I sit in my recliner by the window with the curtain up. I read until about four in the morning, and that Dodge Charger never left until this morning." Wellsy nodded.

My theory exploded in my face. "I see. Well, thank you for your time."

"Come back anytime." Earl smiled. "Friday night is steak night."

I walked back to my car feeling disappointed and confused.

"Now what?" I picked up my cell phone to call the quilt store.

The phone rang and rang. Why wasn't Weenie answering the phone? Surely she couldn't have that many customers?

Unease snaked up my spine.

I started the car and raced out of the RV park. I dialed Dean's number only to have it go to voicemail.

I left him a not-so-nice message about getting to the store ASAP and then gunned it to town.

When I pulled into the parking lot, I spotted Weenie's car. I calmed myself and got out of the car.

I had made a big deal out of nothing. Smiling, I open the door and call out, "Weenie, you're not going to believe…"

I stopped in my tracks when I saw the condition of the store.

Bolts of fabric were tossed around on the floor, and the cash register was opened with the accounting books flung open on the counter.

"Weenie! Where are you?" I raced to the back of the building and came to a grinding halt when I spotted the droplets of blood on the floor.

CHAPTER 26

My head spun and nausea rose in the back of my throat. I grabbed the countertop and slammed my eyes shut. I pulled out my phone and forced my eyes open to focus.

I dialed Dean's number.

He answered on the first ring.

"Dove, you've got…" His voice is laced with irritation.

"I need you at the quilt shop." I slammed my eyes shut to stop my head from spinning.

"Dove, what's wrong? Are you okay?"

"There's blood on the floor and Weenie is missing. I need you," I repeated.

"Weenie?"

I nodded. "Yes, she was watching the store while I went to talk to Polly and Louie."

"Dove. You know better…"

"Dean, not right now. I need you here. Something bad has happened."

"I'm on my way." He ended the call but not before I could hear the blare of his sirens.

I stared at the ceiling and tried to calm my heart. Dean was on his way. Help was on the way. I tried to remind myself that everything was going to be okay.

My cell phone rang and I pulled it out of my pocket, taking a few slow deep breaths.

"Hello?"

"Dove? It's Samantha. From the pharmacy."

As if my day couldn't get any worse. "Samantha, I can't talk right…."

"I'm sorry to call like this but I can't get in touch with Dean."

"He's on his way over here. There's been an emergency." I hoped she'll end the call and leave me alone.

"Oh no. Well, I'm not supposed to tell you, but since he's headed over there. Can you let him know I found the name of the pill he asked me to analyze."

I gasped. "You did?"

"Yes. It's specific for someone with CHF or congestive heart failure. It's fairly new. And there's only one person in Harland Creek that gets that pill."

"Did you say congestive heart failure?"

"Yes." She continued to talk. It sounded almost like white noise in my ears.

My brain began to swim, not from the sight of blood, but from what Samantha Vaughn has just confirmed.

"Dove?"

"Yes?"

"I said, will you tell Dean what I told you? And please don't let anyone know I divulged a patient's private information."

"Of course not." I heard the sirens on the police car as it neared the quilt shop. "Dean is almost here. I'll let him know what you told me. And Samantha?"

"Yes?"

I put my pride aside and forced the next few words out of my mouth. "Dean's a good man. I hope you know that and treat him well." I ended the call.

I figured if I was going to die today trying to save Weenie, I'd want Dean to be happy.

CHAPTER 27

"Why are we going to see Margie Earle? What does she have to do with any of this?" Dean cut his eyes at me.

I chewed the inside of my cheek as my gut tied itself into a knot. "I have a question for her. I think she's going to be able to tell us who the killer is."

"Margie Earle? Why she can barely get out of bed. What kind of information would she possibly have?"

The second Dean pulled up to the front of Margie Earle's house I jumped out and raced up the steps to the porch. I tried the knob but it was locked. I banged on the door. "Mrs. Earle! I need you to open the door."

Dean bounded up behind and looked at me. "She's not answering."

"Break it in." I stated.

He hesitated for a fraction of a second but then braced himself as he plowed into the door.

The door didn't budge. He plowed into it a second time.

The wood splintered around the frame and gave way. He stumbled inside. "Mrs. Earle. It's Dean from the police department."

"Help me," a frail voice called from a room down the hall.

I ran toward the voice and when I got to the room, Dean grabbed my arm. "Let me go in first."

I nodded and watched as he carefully entered the room.

Margie Earle was laying on the floor.

Dean knelt beside her and helped her to a sitting position. "Mrs. Earle, are you alright?"

"Yes, where's Patricia? I've been calling for her for hours to help me get my bath. She always comes."

"I'll call the ambulance." I looked at Dean and he nodded.

I quickly made the call. Before I hung up, I could hear the sirens in the distance.

"Where is Patricia?" Margie gave me a worried look. "She's not on that computer of hers, is she? Sometimes she spends all night talking to someone. She wears headphones so sometimes she can't hear me." Margie huffed.

"Mrs. Earle, do you take a medication for congestive heart failure?" I asked.

She blinked. "Why, yes I do. It's an experimental drug, but the doctor has high hopes it will help me significantly."

I looked at Dean. "That's the pill that was found with Gertrude."

He narrowed his eyes at me. "How do you know?"

"Samantha called and told me."

He pressed his lips into a thin line and gave me a look.

"She tried calling you but couldn't reach you. I told her I would let you know."

Dean looked back at Margie. "Mrs. Earle, you said you can't find Patricia. How long have you been calling for her?"

"At least a couple of hours."

The puzzle pieces were slipping into place. "I'm going to look in Patricia's room."

Just as I entered Patricia's room, I could hear the paramedics enter the house.

I opened Patricia's computer. It was locked.

Ugh, what could she possibly use as her password.

I typed in the word *love*, but that wasn't correct.

I typed in the word *romance*, but again that password was incorrect.

I looked around the room. My eyes landed on the colorful painting of the sunset and what I had thought was a temple. I stepped closer to have a better look. It looked more like a mosque. Like one you would see in India.

I blinked and then walked over to the computer to sit down.

I typed in the word India.

Thankfully the password was correct.

"What are you doing?" Dean came up behind me.

My finger's flew over the keyword as I pulled up Patricia's Facebook page. "How's Margie?"

"She's fine. A little dehydrated but they are taking her to the hospital to get checked out." He leaned over my shoulder. "What are you looking at?"

I clicked the enter button. Patricia's Facebook messages popped up. "This." I sat back in the chair.

"It's from someone named Prince Admad Patel." I scrolled through the conversations exchanged between them. "She actually thought she was talking to a Prince in India."

"That's pretty common among older women. They get lonely and are easy targets for a scam." Dean pointed to one conversation. "Look, it says he needs money so he can fly over to the States to meet her."

"If he's a Prince he should be loaded." I narrowed my eyes and kept scrolling through messages. "Dean, look. He's asked Patricia for money for a long time now. Every time she sends money, he says something else came up and he needs more money." I looked over my shoulder at him.

Dean frowned. "But how is Patricia sending all that money? She can't be making that much at your mom's store. I wonder if she's stealing it from her own mom?"

"Go downstairs and ask Margie before they load her up in the ambulance."

Dean bounded down the stairs while I sat at the computer.

The pill found at the scene belonged to Margie Earle.

Mom was having money problems at the quilt shop so she couldn't have been giving Patricia extra money.

Dean came back into the room. "Margie says she manages her own money. She said that Patricia may be her daughter, but she doesn't have the sense to manage money."

I looked at him. "Patricia is stealing it alright. Just not from her mother. Dean, I know who killed Gertrude. And I know where Weenie is."

CHAPTER 28

"Why are we going to the old Randal cabin? " Dean cut his eyes at me across the seat of the police car. I cringed at Tarzan's hot breath across my neck as we raced along the country road.

"Because I think that's where Weenie is being held. Dean, I was wrong about the killer. It's not Louie or Polly."

"I could have told you that. Louie wasn't even in Harland Creek around the time of Gertrude's death. He was at the RV park with Polly. Seems like they have a thing going on."

I gritted my teeth. "You could have shared that bit of information with me."

"You're not on the police force and you're not privy to investigation details." He countered as he made a sharp turn onto a dirt road. The overgrown weeds covered the rural road, making it impossible to see. But

Dean drove down it like he knew it like the back of his hand.

"Are you mad that Samantha told me about the pill?" I glanced at him.

His eyes narrowed slightly. "No, but I wish she would have told me. She didn't have a right to discuss information pertaining to a case."

I could see the old cabin in the distance. "We should park here and sneak up."

"You're not sneaking anywhere. You're staying right here." He glared as he got out of the car. He opened the back door and let Tarzan out.

Ignoring him, I slid out of the car as well.

"Dove, for once in your life will you listen to me?" He rounded the car and grabbed me by my arms. "I want you to stay here so you won't get hurt." His glare is so intense it almost frightens me.

"Weenie is in there. And I'm going to do everything I can to help her. Even if it involves me getting hurt."

He tightened his grip on my arms. "I can't do this again, Dove. I lost you once, I can't bear losing you again. Look, I contacted the authorities in New York. They confirmed everything you said. I'm sorry I didn't believe you. And I'm sorry you thought I wouldn't understand if you told me the truth. I think that was always our problem. We aren't good when it comes to communicating."

Stunned, I can't speak. That certainly wasn't what I was expecting Dean to say.

"What about Samantha," I wanted to ask, but I

refrained. Instead, I shook my head. "We'll talk about this later. Right now, Weenie is in trouble and we have to do something."

"Fine but stay behind me." Dean shot me another warning look. He released me and gave Tarzan a command to follow.

As we made our way through the overgrown brush around the house, I wished I had worn jeans that day. Limbs and weeds brushed against my legs, scratching my skin.

Dean looked over at me and motioned that he was going around the back of the house to hopefully get the jump on Weenie's kidnapper.

I hid behind a large tree, straining my ears to hear something…anything.

A gunshot echoed in the cabin, followed by a woman's scream.

"Weenie." Ignoring my promise to Dean, I raced for the house.

CHAPTER 29

I burst through the front door and froze.

Patricia was holding a gun pointed directly at Dean and Weenie. Tarzan was whimpering on the floor.

"Don't move, Dove, or I'll put a bullet in you like that dog."

My eyes widened. "You shot Tarzan?"

Patricia narrowed her eyes. "He tried to attack me." She waved the gun toward Dean. "And you, slide that gun over here nice and easy or your girlfriend gets the next bullet."

Dean glared, set his gun on the floor and kicked it towards Patricia.

Patricia bent down to pick up the gun. Fear crept up my spine. Now the woman was holding two guns on us.

"I have to hand it to you, Patricia, I wasn't expecting you to be the killer."

Patricia smiled manically. "What gave me away?"

"A few things. The first clue was the pill found where Gertrude was murdered. Turns out it was your mother's pill, and your mother is the only one in Harland Creek taking that medication. You said when we first met that you were your mother's caretaker. Not only would that mean you take her to her doctor's appointments, but you would also pick up her medicine. The night you killed Gertrude the pill fell out of your purse."

Patricia's eyes hardened. "Gertrude was just like my mother. Always interfering. Always criticizing. If you hadn't come back to town, none of this would have happened."

"Me?"

"Yes. No one works late at the quilt shop. I went in there to put back the money I had borrowed from Mildred. I knew you would be snooping around and find out I had borrowed."

I nodded slowly. "I have to say the fake letter you got from the killer was a nice touch. It certainly has put any suspicion off of you."

Patricia lifted her chin and smirked. "You're not as dumb as you look, Dove."

I glared. "You've been stealing from the shop for months now. And that's why mom's business finances are so bad. When I saw that Weenie was missing and the accounting books were spread out on the counter, I knew that Weenie had been going over the books." I lifted my chin. "What made you look at the books, Weenie?"

"Mildred called me from the hospital. She wanted me to double check that Cindy Hiloff had paid for her quilt in cash. When I went to look, I noticed that a lot of cash payments from clients were missing." Weenie glared at Patricia. "Why would you steal from Mildred? She has treated you better than your own mother."

"Because she's sending money to a man who claims to be a Prince online." I looked at Patricia.

"It's a scam, girl." Weenie glared.

"It's not a scam. He's rich. He just can't access his bank account. He has promised to pay me back once he's in the United States. I'm finally getting married. After all this time, I'm getting married."

I pointed at her. "You murdered Gertrude because she saw you come in the shop that night. She saw you putting the money back and she realized you had stolen from Mom."

"That old bat should have kept her mouth shut. But she kept on and on. Just like Mother." She threatened to tell the whole town I was a thief." Patricia's eyes grew wild as she recounted the night of the murder.

I glanced over at Dean who had knelt beside Tarzan. He slowly stood, taking a step closer to Patricia as she spoke.

"I had taken my large bag inside with me. I'd gotten Mother's oxygen tank refilled earlier so it was still in there. After Gertrude threatened me, she went back to the quilt room to take that teacup quilt. The nerve. She was just going to take it and not pay. And her, calling me a thief! I grabbed the oxygen tank and hit her on the head. I just wanted her to stop talking. She talks all the time. Just like Mother. When I hit her, she spun around and fell to the floor. Hard. Mother's medicine spilled out of the bag. I tried picking them all up. I must have missed one. But I'm not going to miss any of you. You shouldn't have been so nosy, Dove. Now you'll all have to die." She aimed the gun at my head.

"Not today, Satan!" Agnes Jackson came barreling through the door, wearing a beekeeper hat and armed with a baseball bat.

Patricia was so stunned she didn't have time to react. Petunia bleated and head-butted Patricia in the stomach. She doubled over, clutched her chest and dropped the gun to the ground.

"I can't breathe." She searched for her inhaler in the pocket of her jogger.

Dean recovered all the guns and after giving Patricia a hit on her inhaler, handcuffed her.

I went over to where Weenie was sitting down and knelt beside her. "Are you okay?"

Weenie nodded.

I looked at Agnes. "How did you know where we were?"

Agnes pulled her hat off. "I was on the phone with Weenie, and she told me about the discrepancy in the books. I heard Patricia come in and start a commotion. I overheard Patricia say she was taking Weenie to the Randal cabin."

"Backup is on the way." Dean said as he looked all of us over.

I stood and went over to Tarzan. "How is he? Will he be okay?"

"He'll be fine. Thankfully I put his bulletproof vest on him. It stopped the bullet, just hurts like heck." Dean knelt down and patted the dog. Petunia came over and licked the dog's face.

Tarzan eyed Petunia with caution and growled.

"Maybe you should get her away from him." Dean looked at me.

"Yeah. Not sure how he feels about goats." I grabbed her collar, pulling her over to Agnes and Weenie.

I looked at Weenie and Agnes. "I don't know about you two, but I'm so glad this mystery is solved." I sighed and sat down on the floor.

Petunia let out a bleat and everyone laughed.

CHAPTER 30

I lingered at the counter in the back room of the shop, sipping my coffee and reading the newspaper.

For the last few days, I didn't bother getting up early to go into the quilt shop. I was mentally and physically tired from all the excitement of the case.

Patricia was being held for the murder of Gertrude Brown. Patricia's mother, Margie, was stunned at the lengths her daughter went through to find a man. Margie also paid Mom back all the money Patricia had stolen from the shop. Apparently, Margie was a wealthy woman who had made her money through the stock market. No wonder she wouldn't let Patricia handle her finances. Since she couldn't take care of herself, Margie decided to go to an assisted living facility in Jackson.

My cell phone rang just as I was about to read the comics.

"Hello?"

"Dove Agnew? This is Detective Grimes."

I straightened. "Hello, Detective." The last time we spoke was in an interrogation room, and he wasn't at all pleasant.

"I'm calling to let you know that your money is no longer frozen."

"Does this mean you found Cal?"

"We haven't. It seems he has dropped off our radar. Don't worry, we are still checking all leads we get on him."

I let out a breath and nodded. "I see. Well, thank you for letting me know."

He ended the call without saying goodbye. I shook my head.

I would get online to check my bank balance, but I was pretty sure it would be enough to catch Mom up on all her bills and then some.

With a weight lifted off my shoulders, I headed into the quilting room where the women were setting up for their quilting bee.

I looked at the whiteboard and picked up the eraser.

Winston. AKA Courthouse Steps. The quilting ladies had decided to help him get clean. Lorraine called her medical contacts and got him into rehab the day after Patricia was arrested.

I erased his name from the board.

Polly O'Hara. AKA House That Jack Built. Polly was leaving for Florida at the end of the week. Louie was helping her with a nice apartment on the beach. She had called the quilt shop earlier to let me know she had finished her cozy mystery and was feeling better about life in general.

I was happy for her. I erased her name as well.

Eleanor Simmons. AKA Drunkard's Path. Eleanor was still mean as a bat and no one was going to change that. She did seem a bit disappointed that I hadn't been arrested for the crime. But she also said that she wasn't surprised about Patricia being the murderer. She said she trusts no one.

I erased Eleanor's name.

Wendy Rutherford. AKA Pinwheel. Wendy was hanging around Harland Creek for a bit longer. She had made an offer to Louie to buy Gertrude's land, just so no one would harvest the gravel off of it. Louie was still considering the offer.

I erased Wendy's name from the board.

Louie AKA Monkey Wrench.

Louie had inherited everything from Gertrude Brown. He was currently managing all the properties he had inherited. The whole town was hoping he would sell everything and move to Florida with Polly. So far, he was still hanging around.

I erased Louie's name off the board.

"You going to erase your name too, Dove?" Agnes chuckled.

"Yes." I grinned and looked at my name

Dove Agnew. AKA Dove in the Window.

I'd come back to town when I had nowhere else to go. After the past few weeks of getting to know the quilting ladies better, I had started missing my old life less and less every day. I still had no idea what I was going to do next or where I was going to go. But I figured I would stay in Harland Creek a little longer, until I had it all figured out.

I erased my name off the board.

"I can't find Petunia?" Elizabeth looked around the room.

"I'll go find her. Want me to bring her in here?" I asked.

"Please Dove." Elizabeth gave me a grateful smile as she sat in her chair around the quilt they were hand quilting today.

I headed to the front of the store where the closed sign was still visible to the outside world. Mom decided to close on Thursdays so the quilting group could have all day to quilt. Since she'd recovered her money from Margie, she could afford to do that.

When I didn't see the goat in the store, I searched the room where we kept the quilts and then the back room where the coffee was.

I was starting to get worried until I went into Mom's office. Petunia had nudged open the closet and pulled out the Tea Cup Quilt. She was laying down chewing on one of the handkerchiefs.

"Oh no." I tugged the quilt out of the goat's mouth. The quilt ripped.

"Ugh." I sighed, sat on the floor and looked at the rip. I examined the rip and tugged out the handkerchief. "What is this?"

The handkerchief was folded, and I realized for the first time that something was sewed inside the handkerchief. I'd not noticed before because Gertrude was standing over me and barking orders at me as I was loading the quilt into the longarm machine.

I opened the drawer of Mom's desk and finally found what I was looking for. A seam ripper.

I quickly ripped out the seam and spread the handkerchief on the floor.

I gasped as I read what was sewn inside the handkerchief.

Eleanor Simmons broke into Sylvia's store at night. She wanted to buy that building and RV park.

Polly O'Hara used a ghostwriter for her books.

Louie wanted in New York for assault and battery

Wendy Rutherford- wanted gravel deal with Dexter Gravel.

Winston sold drugs.

I looked up after I had read all the secrets that Gertrude had collected on people. Some were true. Some were lies.

I looked over at Petunia. I held out the handkerchief with the words that could destroy so many lives.

Petunia let out a bleat and began devouring the handkerchief.

I decided that I would fix the quilt later and then hang it on the wall.

After Petunia finished her snack, I walked her back into the room where the quilting ladies were sitting in a circle.

"Come on, Dove. We saved you a seat." Weenie patted the chair beside her. All the ladies looked up and smiled.

I might not know where I'm headed in life, but at that moment, I have a place beside some of the finest women I know.

I sat down between Weenie and Mom, picked up my needle, and made the first stitch.

ABOUT THE AUTHOR

Jodi Allen Brice is a USA Today best-selling author of over thirty novels. She writes small town romance, cozy mystery and women's fiction under Jodi Allen Brice.

Check out her website for her upcoming releases and book signings! jodiallenbrice.com

ALSO BY JODI ALLEN BRICE

Harland Creek Series
Promise Kept
Promise Made
Promise Forever
Christmas in Harland Creek
Promise of Grace
Promise of Hope
Promise of Love

Laurel Cove Series
Lakehouse Promises
Lakehouse Secrets
Lakehouse Dreams

Stand alone novels.
So This Is Goodbye
Not Like the Other Girls (2023)

Harland Creek Cozy Mystery Quilters
Mystery of the Tea Cup Quilt
Mystery of the Drunkards Path Quilt (2023)
Mystery of the Grandmother's Garden Quilt (2023)

Manufactured by Amazon.ca
Bolton, ON